Killings in Horse Country

by

Augie Salzer

DORRANCE
PUBLISHING CO
EST. 1920
PITTSBURGH, PENNSYLVANIA 15238

Dorrance Publishing Co
585 Alpha Drive
Pittsburgh, PA 15238
Visit our website at www.dorrancebookstore.com

ISBN: 979-8-89211-286-4
eISBN: 979-8-89211-784-5

Dedication:

To my family, the Robertsons, and my husband, Jim, for all their invaluable assistance and encouragement.

Chapter 1

"9-1-1, what's your emergency?"

"A man is lying on the horse trail next to 150th Street."

"Is he hurt?"

"I don't know, but he's not moving."

"Exactly where on the horse trail is the man?" the dispatcher asked as she typed the information into the computer.

"He's closer to the C.R. 328 entrance."

"Okay, what's your name? Hello? Hello? Are you still there?"

With all the information available, Detective Grant Steele responded to the scene with lights and sirens. Within minutes, he found the man and noticed the blood on the back of his head.

"Dispatch, we need the coroner out here. And send CSI Jack Wagner too," Steele said on his radio.

"They're on the way."

Steele walked over the brown, trampled grass, looking for clues in the thick bushes, tall pines, and cedar trees surrounding the trail, aware not to step on the body. The tall, thick trees block out most of the sun. In the dim light, he noticed a cell phone in the grass, carefully picked it up with two fingers so as not to ruin any fingerprints, and put it in an evidence bag. He sees a small piece of bright red paper and puts it in another evidence bag.

Wagner arrives, swatting flies away from his face.

"I can't believe there are so many flies. Okay, what do you have for me?"

"The body is small, like a young boy, but his face shows he's older," Steele said, giving him two evidence bags, one with the cell phone and one holding a small piece of red paper.

"What's this?" Wagner asks.

"I don't know. I found it in the bushes, but it may have something to do with the dead man," he said. "Let me know what it is when you figure it out. His flip phone was open like he was talking or texting."

"The only evidence of this man's death is the blood on the rock under the back of his head. He has no defensive wounds, and his clothes are clean, so he wasn't in a fight. He also doesn't have any identification on him," Wagner said examining the body. "His pockets are empty. He doesn't have any I.D. on him."

"Could it have been a robbery?"

"No, he still has his watch and a ring on his finger. Otherwise, it looks like the body we found on the trail closer to the S.R. 40 entrance last week," Wagner said, checking the body. "His liver temp shows he died about three hours ago, probably between 7 a.m. and 10 a.m. Did you find anything else?"

"I'm looking, but I only found the phone and that piece of red paper, but these flies are annoying, and it's hot. Let's finish and get out of here."

"It's warm for the middle of November. Watch out that you don't step in the horse apples," Wagner says.

"The what?"

"Clumps of horse dung are called horse apples, and you're about to step in it."

"You always amaze me. How do you know about things like this?" Steele asks.

"Simple. I spent my childhood on a farm with my grandparents and learned all about that stuff. This clump looks fresh, which is probably why there are so many flies."

"Okay, finish taking your pictures and get his fingerprints so we can get out of this heat."

Ashley Parker, the new reporter for the *Ocala Star Banner*, approaches the scene. She is holding a handkerchief soaked with perfume to block the smell of the horse poop.

"Hi, gentlemen. I heard you both transferred here last month from the Villages, and I wondered when I would run into you," Ms. Parker said.

"It's good to see you, Ashley. How did you find us?"

"Your red and blue lights shine through the gaps in the trees. It's like a beacon beckoning me down the road."

"Why did you decide to move here?" she asks them.

"We heard there were fantastic job openings for us here at the Marion County Sheriff's Office, and we couldn't pass up the opportunity, so here we are," Steele said.

"Good for both of you. Do you have any info about the body you found?" Ashley asks.

"Right now, we don't have anything. You'll have to wait until the coroner's report. Why weren't you at last week's discovery of a body on the other end of the trail?" Steele asks.

"I was on vacation and didn't hear about it until today. Can you give me anything on the body found last week?"

"You'll have to wait until the coroner's report. We should have it next week," he said with a smirk.

"Okay. Also, thanks for giving me that scoop on the Villages' serial killings in the alley. After the article appeared in the paper, I received a great job offer from the Ocala newspaper. I accepted their offer and moved here six months ago," Ashley says as she leaves.

"Oh, good. The M.E.'s assistant is finally here, and Wagner and I are also leaving. You can check out the fingerprints and let me know what the red paper is as soon as you figure it out," Steele asks Wagner as they leave.

"With such a small piece, that will be a challenge."

"I'm confident that you will figure it out."

Chapter 2

Tommy Cobb, eldest of three brothers, drove his shiny red Ford F-250 two-door truck with flames painted on the front of the vehicle and lots of chrome and dark tinted windows into a thick cluster of bushes and tall pine trees on an abandoned road. The scent of pine is strong. He is careful not to scratch his pride and joy.

"Are you in the right spot?" Doug asks.

"I've parked in this same spot for the last seven days, little brother. Of course, I'm in the right spot. I'm parked right in the middle of all the trash you guys have been throwing on the ground," Tommy said. "You should pick up all the wrappers and cans before someone gets you guys for littering."

"Will you guys be quiet? I want to see if I can hear what they're saying, but I think we're too far away. It looks like there are a lot of people at the ranch today. I wonder what's going on?" Steve, the middle brother, asks.

"Give me the binoculars so I can see what's happening. I also want to see if anyone moved the horse trailers," Tommy said, putting down the tinted windows.

"As you can see, the people are saddling their horses and taking them out of the stable. It looks like they are taking them for a ride because most riders are heading toward the horse trail. The three horse trailers are still next to the barn," Steve said.

"I can see that all eight stalls are empty, the harnesses are not on the hooks outside the stall, and the tack door is wide open. There are two people with their horses still outside the barn, but all the rest of the horses are gone. I guess you're right. They're just taking their horses for a Sunday afternoon ride on the trail," Tommy says.

"I'm getting in the back and having my lunch," Doug says as he climbed into the truck's bed.

"If you would have been up early so we could've gotten here by 7:30 a.m. as usual, then maybe we would know what was going on," Tommy said.

"At least we can watch the riders going to the horse trail instead of just sitting here and doing nothing," Steve said.

"You can always come back here and watch the clouds and look for birds with me," Doug said, shading his eyes from the sun.

"Don't eat all the food, Doug, 'cause we still have to stay here until we see if the lady leaves again and when she comes back. I don't want you complaining later that you are hungry 'cause we can't leave until we finish this job today," Tommy said.

"Well, it doesn't look like the lady is gonna leave at 3 p.m. cause it's almost 3 p.m. now, and it will be dark soon. Maybe she doesn't go anywhere on Sundays. Besides, we've been here a week. When are you gonna report to the boss? I'm getting bored sitting out here every day just watching the clouds in the sky," Doug, the youngest, said, munching on a sandwich.

"You know the boss hired us to watch and report on the activities of this barn after a week. So, I'll text him today with everything we've seen so far."

Tommy texts all the findings of the last week to the boss before they leave for the day.

"After telling him about our week, the boss texted back that he wants us to stake out the ranch for another week to see if there are any new changes and then report to him again," Tommy said.

Slapping his forehead with his palm, Doug says. "Oh, no. I can't stay out here for another week. It's way too boring. Even the clouds are boring, and I haven't seen a bird all day."

"We're gonna get paid good money when we finish this job. So just settle down and stop complaining. Think about all the money we will get for doing nothin' except sitting here all day. Now, just be quiet," Tommy said.

"For all the sitting around and doing nothing, we better be getting a whole lot of money, and I can't wait to spend it."

Chapter 3

After a forty-mile ride to Leesburg, Steele finds the medical examiner's office. His GPS guides him to the light-yellow colored building. The two-story building has a large asphalt parking lot with many trees that shade the parked cars. A roofed structure extends from the main entrance, allowing vehicles to pass under it.

"Hi Doc, I had a difficult time finding you down here."

"The neighbors don't like the idea of a morgue in their neighborhood, so the city put me out here."

"Have you finished the autopsies on the two men from the trail?"

"Sure, I finished the second one just before lunch."

"Great, tell me what you found."

"Well, the first body's cause of death was a broken neck, and somebody broke his spine. He was approximately thirty-nine years old, four-foot-ten, and weighed 110 pounds. He was probably a jockey because he has fragile bones from long-term dietary abuse and tooth erosion, probably from constantly throwing up. He also has kidney disease, a characteristic of jockeys," the doctor said.

"What makes you think he was a jockey?"

"Basically, because of his size and his BMI is too low, showing he is underweight. Jockeys must keep their weight at a certain level to be able to race. Did you know that Ocala is the horse capital of the world, and we have a lot of jockeys living and working here?"

"No, I didn't know that. Now, what about the other body we found on the trail?"

"The second victim from the horse trail was probably also a jockey since he had the same problems of fragile bones and terrible teeth as the first body. This one is about forty-one years old. He is five feet tall and weighs 112 pounds. His cause of death was a fractured head. I'm going to say somebody, or something caused both men to be thrown from their horses, which easily broke their bones, causing their deaths, but you're the detective, not me."

"Thanks for your help, Doc. I will check with Wagner to see if he has the results of the fingerprints yet."

Steele drove down S.R. 40 to the Marion County Sheriff's Office and jail complex and walked into Wagner's office, two rooms down from his office.

The large windowless room has a table, a computer, a microscope, pieces of examination equipment, and various other analysis equipment. A large screened area with shelves and racks for evidence storage is in the corner. The wire evidence door has a combination lock and a clipboard attached to the screen to record the incoming evidence and the people entering the area.

Steele's office is more prominent than his previous office in the Villages. His room has a large window overlooking the parking lot. The walls are a light beige, and he has a desk with a computer and two visitor chairs. His three-drawer file cabinet is still relatively empty since he has only worked here for two months.

"Hey, Wagner, do you have any information about the horse trail bodies?"

"Sure, I was about to call you."

"Okay, what do you have for me?"

"The first body was Kyle Adams, and the second was Jimmy Sparks. They were both licensed as jockeys. I matched the prints from their applications," Wagner said, checking his computer.

"Great work. The doc said they were probably jockeys because of their size and the terrible condition of their bodies. Did you figure out what the red paper was?"

"Sure. I've got an answer for you. But you aren't going to believe what it is."

"Well, don't keep me in suspense. What is it?" Steele asks.

"The paper had potassium nitrate, charcoal, and sulfur on it."

"It sounds like gun powder to me. So, what is it?" Steele asks.

"I checked it out, and it was a firecracker with the brand name Black Cat. You know, they are the tiny red cylinder-shaped firecrackers with the wick to light and are sold sixteen to a package. It also makes a loud pop sound. The sound probably spooked the horse and knocked off its rider."

"That's great. That will classify this as murder. We have to figure out how the first fatality occurred," Steele said.

"It looks like we may have a serial killer on our hands."

"No. It takes three or more killings to say we have a serial killer. We should also find out what happened to the horses they were riding."

"That's a good point," Wagner said.

Chapter 4

"Have you canvased the ranches around the horse trail yet?" Wagner asks.

"I was heading out there now. Do you want to come along?"

"Sure, my work is all finished for today, and it would be good to get out for a while, and maybe we can find a place for Thanksgiving dinner," Wagner said.

"I checked out a map of the area, and there are four ranches by the horse trail. The first is the Black House of Dominoes Thoroughbred Farms, 550 acres owned by Laura and Edward Moore. We can start with them," Steele said.

After they traveled for a few minutes past several acres of lush green grass with horses grazing on S.R. 40, they noticed the ranch was just past the Marion County 'Farmland Preservation Area' sign on the side of C.R. 328. They find the ornamental black wrought iron gate at the entrance with two large dominos overhead at the beginning of Moore's farm is open.

They cruise the curving driveway with tall pine trees on each side of the driveway. A decorative wood fence with brick fence posts surrounds the front of the property. They walk up two steps and rings the doorbell. A maid opens the door.

"My name is Detective Grant Steele and this is CSI Wagner from the Marion County Sheriff's Office," as he showed his badge and ID. "We would like to speak with Mr. Moore.

"Come in. Please wait, and I will tell him you are here."

They smelled the mouth-watering aroma of a Thanksgiving turkey cooking as they entered.

A large man with receding gray hair, about five foot ten inches tall, weighing 200 pounds, and wearing jeans, a flannel shirt, and cowboy boots entered the room a few minutes later.

"Good afternoon, gentlemen. My name is Ed Moore. How can I help you?"

"My name is Detective Grant Steele, and this is CSI Jack Wagner from the Marion County Sheriff's Office," as he showed him his badge and I.D. "Sorry to bother you on Thanksgiving, but we want to ask you some questions about two men we found on the horse trail recently."

"That's okay. Our dinner won't be ready for a while. By chance, could one of the men be Jimmy Sparks or Kyle Adams?" Moore asks.

"Yes, that is the names of the men we found. Why do you ask?"

"Well, Jimmy and Kyle have been with me for several years. They were my best jockeys when I first started racing my thoroughbreds. They are now retired and help around the farm, but they haven't been around for a few days, and I wondered what happened to them," Moore said.

"Have they gone missing before?" Steele asks.

"Yes, they habitually wander off for a few days and then return."

"Did you report them missing this time?"

"No, I didn't report them because they have done this several times in the last couple of years. They would leave for a week or so, then come back. So, I wasn't concerned about them."

"Did Sparks or Adams have gambling or drinking problems or have any enemies?"

"No, they didn't have any problems. They were both hard workers, and everyone liked them."

"Are there a lot of jockeys in the area?" Steele asks.

"You must be new to the area," Moore said.

"Yes, we are. Why do you ask?"

"In 2007, the city council officially named Ocala and Marion County the horse capital of the world, a testament to the county's unique involvement in all things equestrian. We also have a record of producing some of the finest champions in the sport. Ocala has the most horses and several international horse shows, champion race horses, and public riding trails. Ocala has more horses than any other county in the United States," Moore said proudly. "Florida's first horse-breeding pioneers knew the limestone under Ocala's soil allowed for building good roads and strong horses. "

"We didn't know that. I thought Kentucky was the place with all the horses, not Ocala," Steele said.

"Kentucky is known primarily for thoroughbreds, but Florida is home to many different breeds. Florida is the place where many horses train in the winter. Also, Ocala has over 400 thoroughbred farms, and mine is one of them. My farm is 550 acres, and we have several thoroughbreds that we are currently training. You should check out WEC when you can," Moore said.

"What is WEC?"

"The World Equestrian Center is located on S.R. 40 west of Ocala. Many horse owners take part in different competitions at WEC, and you could learn a lot about horses there."

"Excuse me, sir, but your wife is requesting you," the maid said entering the room.

"Will you pardon me, gentlemen, but my wife is sickly and confined to her bed. You should go to WEC next week. We're having a town hall meeting there next Thursday at 5 p.m. You can meet the other ranchers." Moore said as he turned to leave.

"Excuse me, Mr. Moore, just one more question. Are you missing any horses?"

"I don't know. We have so many horses on the ranch, and I don't keep a count of every horse. Let me check with my ranch foreman, and I will let you know."

"Thank you for your time. We'll be at the meeting," Steele said as he gave him his business card.

Steele and Wagner drove around Ocala, passing numerous horse farms in rolling green pastures. They looked for a restaurant open for dinner on Thanksgiving day. After a while, they noticed a sign announcing the Hilton hotel was serving Thanksgiving dinner.

Enjoying their turkey dinner with all the trimmings, Steele confides in Wagner and tells him that Nancy Jennings, head of police investigations in the Villages, is visiting for Christmas week.

"That is wonderful. Where is Nancy going to stay?"

"I'm making a reservation at the Comfort Inn & Suites hotel in Dunnellon for her," Steele said. "Why do you ask?"

"Well, seeing her and catching up on everything since we left would be nice. Maybe we can all get together for dinner one night while she is here," Wagner said.

"Sounds like a great plan."

Chapter 5

Steele and Wagner checked out some of the ranchers before attending the town hall meeting scheduled for the first week in December. They entered the private meeting room filled with ranchers just before the tall, slender Lt. Governor arrived wearing a charcoal business suit, white silk blouse, dark gray high heels, and a Coach purse. She tosses her shoulder-length, straight brown hair as she walks. As she enters the room, two large security guards with military haircuts wearing black suits, white shirts, and black ties are on each side of the Lt. Governor. They wear Ray-Ban sunglasses and have wired security earpieces with the curly cord down the back of their necks.

Frank Green, owner of the Green Oaks Ranch, has agreed to oversee the meeting. He rushes to greet the Lt. Governor, almost tripping over his feet as he escorts her to the podium.

"Everyone sit down, and we will start the meeting," Green said into the microphone. "Please welcome our Lt. Governor Morgan Eastman."

"Greetings, ladies and gentlemen. Welcome to our town hall meeting. I'm here to discuss the proposed Florida Turnpike extension. So far, we are still planning that DOT will build the proposed road in Citrus, Sumter, Levy, and Marion counties," she said. "A copy of the map with the proposed route is set up on the easel for everyone to view."

After hearing the disturbing news, the audience jumped out of their seats and started talking at once, shouting that this will ruin our ranches. Some of the ranchers are checking out the map. The protective security guards moved closer to the Lt. Governor.

"Please, ladies and gentlemen, let's have some control. The committee and I have not decided where DOT will build the road. The governor and I are still holding town hall meetings around the state to hear from the people in all the counties affected," Lt. Governor said. "We still have a lot of data to consider before we make the final decision."

Ashley Parker, the reporter, slid into a seat next to the back door and started taking notes.

"Our land, the Double H Ranch, is only 400 acres, and according to the proposed map, my husband, Howard, and I would lose most, if not all, of our land," Helen Lane said as the vein in her forehead throbbed.

"The new road would destroy large areas of our ranches. This road would also pollute our waterways, destroying the Rainbow Springs, one of the state's largest springs. My wife, Paula, and I are against this project even though, according to the proposed map, we probably won't lose much of our land," David Drake, the Bit of Heaven Thoroughbred ranch owner, said. "Maybe the department of transportation could build the road elsewhere so none of us would lose our lands. We didn't work hard to build our farms so that you could take it for a road no one wants."

The audience is standing, talking, and shoving their fists in the air, and everyone is trying to grab the podium microphone to shout their disapproval to Mrs. Eastman.

The meeting continued for another half hour before the angry, discouraged people stomped out of the room. They were disappointed that the Lt. Governor didn't say somebody would cancel the road and not build it.

Green finally adjourned the meeting when the group was

reduced to five people, and announced they would have another meeting in February.

The Lt. Governor tells her security guards that Mr. Green is taking her to her home in Ocala, and she dismissed them for the day.

"Are you sure, Ma'am? The crowd was unruly today. We don't mind taking you home, and it's still early," one of the guards said.

"It's okay. Enjoy your time off, and you can pick me up in the morning at the usual time."

Wagner and Steele notice Ashley in the back and go sit next to her.

"What do you think about all of this?" Steele asks.

"I understand this has been going on for a couple of years. The ranchers have been upset with everything, but it makes for a good story. Excuse me. I want to go outside and get a good quote from the ranchers before they all leave," Parker said as she quickly left the room, followed by Wagner and Steele.

Parker's story is located on tomorrow's front page telling everyone about the rancher's opposition to the new road extension and another meeting is scheduled for February.

After all the people were gone, and her guards had left, Frank Green approached the Lt. Governor.

"Are you ready? We have dinner reservations in the Stirrups restaurant right here in the hotel," Frank said.

"That would be lovely. Are we going to your home after dinner too?"

"Of course, but first we have to talk about you stopping the proposed road or at least changing the direction. You know the way it is now. It'll wipe out my 100 acres. I can't lose my farm. It is all I have," Frank said, wringing his hands.

"I have always loved you and promised to stop the road going through your land. Now, stop wringing your hands, and let's enjoy dinner and some special time in your bed before you take me home."

"That sounds wonderful. I've missed you," Frank said as he relaxed and escorted her to the dining room.

"Frank. You know I also have to spend a lot of time in my Tallahassee office. But currently, my schedule is allowing me to spend time here until Christmas."

"Is your husband, Ted, still deployed? And will you be able to spend time with me?"

"He has been gone for six months, and I don't expect him back before next year. Of course, I will spend a lot of time with you. Have I ever missed our anniversary day with you before?"

"It is time again for the anniversary of our meeting," he said.

"December 22nd is the first day we saw each other across the room at the political office Christmas party and eventually connected. It has been a breathtaking love that has blossomed since we first met two years ago. It's been an exciting time, and I enjoy every minute with you," she said as they walked into the restaurant.

Chapter 6

Wagner and Steele were working in their offices when the dispatcher notified them of another body found on the horse trail closer to S.R. 40. They rushed to Steele's car and proceeded to the crime scene with blue lights flashing and sirens blaring.

"I guess this makes it three bodies found on the trail, which puts it in the serial killer category," Wagner said.

"Let's wait until we get there and check out the body before we assume that," Steele said.

The patrol vehicle stopped just before the body, and the men checked the area.

"Well, it looks the same as the first two bodies, so I guess we have a serial killer on our hands," Steele said.

"This man is small, so he was probably a jockey too. The way the body is lying there, you don't immediately notice the bullet hole in his chest. He probably has a broken back from the body's position, and it looks like he fell off a horse. There are no defensive wounds, and it wasn't a robbery because there is still a ring on his finger, but I can't find any identification or anything in the pockets. His liver temp and lack of rigor show he died about two hours ago. I turned him over, and he had a hole in his back where the bullet exited the body. It looks like a 9mm, but the lab can confirm that."

"Okay, Wagner, get his fingerprints and some pictures, and I will see if there is any evidence in the area."

"I'm working on it now. I'm cold and want to get back to the warm car, so let me know if you find any evidence or the brass from the gun," Wagner said as he pulled up the collar of his light jacket and turned his back to the wind.

"What's wrong? You are shaking like a leaf and can barely get his fingerprints. I hope the pictures won't be blurry."

"For the end of December, it is one of the coldest days of the year, and I don't have my winter jacket on today. It's cold enough to see my breath, but I'll be okay in the car with the heater on full blast. It was so warm last week. I didn't think it would get this cold today."

"I heard the weatherman last night say we are going to get a winter blast of cold air today, so I dug out my winter clothes, and I'm glad I did," Steele said.

"It isn't usually this cold just before Christmas. I guess it is the climate change everyone is discussing. It's so cold out here. I wonder if we'll get snow this year. I hope the M.E. gets here soon before the body freezes and me too," Wagner said.

"Okay, just get in the car and put on the heater. I want to look around some more. Maybe I will find something."

"You don't have to tell me twice. I'm gone."

Parker arrives, notices the body, and asks Steele about the bullet hole.

"This one is different. Why was this one shot and not the others?"

"That is why we call it an investigation," Steele said as he continued his search of the area and discovered an open flip phone on top of the packed-down grass.

"It's too cold out here. Can I call you tomorrow for more information?" Parker said as she left, pulling her winter coat tight around her.

"You might wait until I get the coroner's report," Steele said as he carefully put the open phone in an evidence bag. He takes the phone to Wagner in the car.

"Great. You found a phone. Did you find any evidence of

fireworks like we found last time?" Wagner asked. "Did you find any shell casings from the gun?"

"No, the perp must have picked up his brass before leaving. We will have to check with the ranchers and see if they know the dead jockey and if they are missing any horses. We must also find out how many ranchers own guns," Steele said. "I received a text from Ed Moore saying he is missing the two quarter horses usually exercised by his two dead jockeys."

"Well, the third jockey will probably belong to one of the other ranchers. Can we stop by my apartment and let me pick up my winter jacket before I freeze out here?" Wagner asks.

"Sure. Then we can visit the Green Oaks Ranch to see if he is missing a jockey and a horse."

Getting Wagner's jacket, scarf, and gloves didn't take long. They stopped for lunch before the men arrived at Mr. Green's property. They quickly noticed his ranch is much smaller than the other ranches they have visited.

Steele rings the doorbell of a tiny home surrounded by two large oak trees and acres of pasture with several horses nibbling on the grass.

"How may I help you?" Frank Green asks.

"My name is Detective Grant Steele, and this is CSI Jack Wagner of the Marion County Sheriff's Office. May we come in?" Steele asked as he showed his badge and identification.

"What is this all about?" Green asked as he opened his door.

"Are you missing a jockey and a horse?"

"Yes, I have several jockeys who helped around the ranch for several years. Willie, my best jockey, left riding one of my quarter horses this morning, but he isn't back yet and should have returned a couple of hours ago. Why do you ask?"

"We found a third body on the trail just before lunch, and he appears to have the appearance of a jockey, but we didn't find a horse," Steele said.

"The horse will return home if the rider gets off the horse and doesn't tie him to a stationary object," Green said.

"Do you own a gun or rifle?"

"Of course, I own a rifle. Why do you ask?"

"It looks like someone shot the jockey, and we want to know if you own a gun?"

"I only have a .22 rifle, but all the ranchers have guns and rifles to protect against wildlife out here."

"Okay. Also, can you go to the morgue in Leesburg and identify the body to see if it's your jockey?"

"I'm sorry, Detective, but I have a lot of work to do and won't be able to go. Isn't there some other way to identify the body?"

"Yes. We can use fingerprints to identify the victim. Thank you for your time," Steele said, and they left.

"Strangely, he didn't seem too concerned about someone killing his employee. It's like he has something else on his mind."

"What could be more important than your dead employee and a missing horse?"

"It would be interesting to find out," Wagner said.

Chapter 7

In the early morning the Cobb brothers head toward their truck when their sister, Sally, goes to the door.

"Where do you think you guys are going, all dressed in your clean clothes?" she asks.

"These are not our clean clothes. These are the same old dirty bib overalls we have worn all week with our worn-out sneakers. You know we have a job to do. I already told you about it, and you will not like it. Remember?" Tommy said.

"Well, I'm going with you. I don't like staying in this rundown trailer all by myself. What if Dad comes back?"

"He's been gone for three years. After all this time, I don't think he's ever coming back. So, just relax. We have left you for over a week, and you've been fine. Now, we have work to do. Besides, we have two neighbors only a quarter of a mile away," Tommy said. "If you have a problem, you can run to them."

"I'm still coming with you. I want some of the money you're getting. Doug, you get in the back. There isn't room for all four of us inside the truck."

"Why am I always the one stuck in the back?" Doug asks.

"Because you are the youngest, and I'm the oldest and have all the food for lunch," Sally said.

After everyone is seated, Tommy drives to their spot to continue surveillance.

After several hours of everyone taking turns looking through the binoculars, the boredom sets in.

"Why do I smell Christmas trees?"

"You silly goose, can't you see all the pine trees surrounding us?" Tommy said.

"You're right. Okay, now when does something happen?" Sally asks.

"It's usually quiet until about 2 p.m., then the lady brings the horses in from the paddock and puts them in their stalls. She removes their bridles and hangs them on the hook outside their stalls. Then, after she puts hay in their stalls, she closes the barn door and leaves," Doug said.

"You mean we have waited all day just to see her put up horses and leave?"

"I told you before it wouldn't be any fun for you, but you didn't listen," Tommy said.

"Okay, I'm ready to go home," she said.

"No, we have to wait and see if the lady leaves as usual and when she comes back before we can leave."

"Well, I have to use the bathroom, so we have to leave."

"Just walk down the path for a while and then go around the corner for a bit and go. That's where we have been going, 'cause we're not leaving," Tommy said.

"Wait. A pickup truck loaded with hay is pulling into the driveway and opens the gate with the keypad. The lady is going out to meet them," Steve said.

They watch the three men in the pickup unload the hay and put it in the barn. Then the woman gives them something, probably money, and they leave.

"That's a lot of hay. Apparently, it's only delivered every other week, because they didn't do that last week on Monday," Tommy said.

"So, this is what you do here? Sitting in a truck all day isn't fun," Sally said after returning to the truck.

"You can sit in the back and watch clouds with me," Doug said.

"Yep, we sit here and watch every day and report to the boss, but this is different from last week. The lady is leaving again at 3 p.m., just like last week," Steve said.

"Okay, make sure you are writing all this down so we don't get mixed up on what day things happened," Tommy said.

"I've been writing everything down every day. Just like you told me to do," Steve said.

"Will we be able to leave when she comes back?" Sally asks.

"That's what I've been telling you all day. Why don't you just listen? We don't leave until she gets back," Tommy said impatiently.

Chapter 8

Paula Drake and Helen Lane have met at their favorite restaurant on the fifteenth of the month for years to have lunch. The ladies arrived at the posh golf course restaurant dressed in their best finery and expensive jewelry.

The waiter, José, greets them at the door.

"Good afternoon, ladies. I have your regular table ready for you," José says as he leads them to the best table overlooking the golf course.

"I almost canceled today because I'm so busy preparing for my Christmas party," Paula said after they were seated.

"We have always gotten together to have lunch and gossip on the fifteenth of each month. You are always busy just before Christmas. Why is this different? But I'm glad you showed up today. I need to talk to you about my problem," Helen said.

"I also have a problem, but first, we need some wine."

José returns to the table with the menu. The ladies look over the extensive menu while Paula flirts with the handsome waiter. They order a glass of Chardonnay.

"Our special today is salmon with a bourbon glaze with rice and seasonal vegetables," José said.

The suggestion sounds good, and both ladies order the salmon from the waiter.

"I'm sorry, Paula. I didn't realize you were having problems.

You always seem so organized and in control."

"I am always in control. Let me get some wine first, and I will tell you about my problem," Paula said. "My husband is trying to lure Willie Flynn, Green's jockey, to work for us and ride our thoroughbred in the upcoming races. The jockey is supposed to be the best around here, and my husband wants him to race our horse in the Kentucky Derby."

"Why doesn't he just give the jockey a lot of money? I'm sure he will take the job then," Helen said.

"My husband doesn't want to make enemies with the other ranchers by luring away their good help, but he will devise a plan to get the jockey. Okay, I've had some wine and am ready to listen. Tell me why you're worried." Paula said.

"My daughter, Cat, is having problems with kidney stones. She has been getting them since she was eighteen. She even went to Miami, Houston, and Tennessee for different studies, and they still can't figure out why she gets the stones," Helen said, rubbing her temples. "One doctor found six tumors on her thyroid, which he said causes kidney stones, and the doctors removed the tumors, but that didn't seem to help. Cat has had numerous lithotripsy to blast the stones to make them smaller to pass. She told me a stone had poked through her urethra, and now she has sepsis. The doctor is giving her strong antibiotics and pain meds because of her sepsis and the pain from kidney stones. He wants to remove her left kidney because the kidney stones are sepsis. She has less energy now, has brain fog, and gets frequent urinary tract infections. I'm so worried about her and don't know what to do," Helen said.

"Okay, can you do anything to help her from here?" Paula asks.

"No, she's in Texas and has a wonderful husband helping her, but I'm still worried. I would like to visit her, but we don't have the money for the plane fare, and Howard can't travel anymore."

"Of course, you're worried. Don't worry about money. I'm going to pay for your lunch like I have been doing since you've had a run of bad luck," Paula said. "Now, just drink your wine, and let me tell you about Laura Moore. This news will get your mind off your daughter. Did you read the Facebook post by Laura?"

"Paula, I don't have time for that nonsense, but tell me about it."

"Well, as usual, she wrote on the internet and told everyone how sick she is and bedridden, but I saw her at the farmer's market Saturday, and she looked fine," Paula said.

"Are you sure it was her?"

"Of course, I'm sure. Laura is probably the only one around here that young. I even talked to her for a few minutes, and she told me she was scheduled to have more medical tests done. I know it was Laura."

"Well, maybe she just had a good day and wanted to get out for a while. You never know," Helen said.

"You always think the best of people. By the way, are you still coming to my Christmas party?" Paula asks.

"You know I wouldn't miss one of your parties. Howard and I will be there as always. Do you need any help?"

"Helen, you are such a good friend. Could you arrive about thirty minutes early to help me set up the drinks?"

"Sure. I've already made a batch of Christmas cookies for your party. And we'll be there with bells on. Howard won't be much help, but he can spend time with David."

"Good. Now, stop worrying about Cat. She has her husband and good doctors taking care of her. You can call her every day and talk again on Christmas day too," Paula said.

"Thanks. I hope you get your problem with the jockey fixed too."

"I'm sure we will have the jockey working for us soon. My husband is a very persuasive man, and he always gets what he wants."

Chapter 9

The medical examiner texts Steele that he completed the third victim's autopsy. Steele used Facetime on the computer to talk to the M.E. to get the autopsy results. He is thankful that Nancy Jennings showed him how to do Facetime before he left so they could speak regularly.

"Hi Doc, tell me some good news. Is the third victim just like the first two?"

"You're almost right, except someone shot this one at close range. From the angle of the shot, I would say the perp was on the ground and shot upward. The autopsy results show he was killed with a 9mm to his heart, causing death instantly. The bullet went through and through and exited his back. He was also a jockey, twenty years old, five foot tall, and weighed 113 pounds. Even at his young age, his bones are becoming brittle, and he has the start of tooth erosion. He also has kidney disease. This one must have been a working Jockey because they are committed to riding and will do anything to keep their weight low to qualify to race. They will binge eat, then purge with laxatives and vomit to avoid gaining weight. Even after they retire, they can't break the addiction of anorexia, which is starving themselves," the M.E. said.

"What about the bullet?"

"You will have to go out there and look for a bullet. Look in the brushes and any trees around the body."

" I guess Wagner and I will go bullet hunting. Then we'll check on the ranchers again to find where this one lived."

Steele went to Wagner's office to find the identity of the latest victim.

"What do you have for me?"

"Hi, Steele. The third victim's fingerprints show that Willie Flynn, a jockey, is our third victim."

"I guess I have to return to the Green Oaks Ranch and talk to Frank Green again. We also have to look for the bullet back at the scene. Do you want to come along?"

"Sure, I like seeing the ranches with all the horses.

The two men returned to the scene. They searched for an hour crawling on the ground looking for the bullet but couldn't find it anywhere.

"Could the perp have taken the time to find the bullet and take it with him?"

"Anything is possible. You said the victim was dead for about two hours, so he would have time to find it. Okay, let's visit Green," Steele said.

The men approached the front door as Frank Green opened it, ready to leave.

"Sorry, gentlemen, but I was about to leave for an appointment. Can we make this fast?"

"It seems that the deceased is Willie Flynn, as you expected. "Did your horse return yet?"

"No, he didn't, but I have to leave. If you need anything else, you can call tomorrow," Green said as he closed the door and left.

"Did you notice the amount of aftershave or cologne he was wearing? Also, he was wearing a western-style sport coat, ironed jeans, shiny cowboy boots, and a black Stetson hat. I wonder what kind of appointment he has?" Steele said.

"He didn't seem too worried about his missing horse or jockey," Wagner said. "He did look better than the last time we saw him, and the aroma around him is stifling."

"I'm curious and wonder where he is going. Maybe we should follow him?

"Sure, just don't get too close. "Wagner said.

"This isn't the first time I've tailed someone. I'll stay back, and Green won't even see us."

They follow the vehicle to a lovely house in the historic district of Ocala and watch Green park his vehicle on the street. He gets out carrying a tall, thin paper bag, walks past three houses before he goes to the next place, and rings the doorbell at the two-story colonial house with a wrap-around porch. Immediately, the Lt. Governor, wearing a robe and slippers, opens the door.

"Did you get the address?"

"We don't need to. Check out who opened the door. Here, you can use my binoculars."

"I didn't expect that. I wonder what's going on?" Steele asks.

"I'm curious what Green was carrying in the bag. It looked like a bottle of wine or maybe champagne."

"I would like to know why he parked so far away when he could have pulled into the empty driveway."

"He probably didn't want anyone to know who he was visiting."

"You have a good point there. Maybe something is going on since he could park in the driveway if they were talking business."

Chapter 10

The Cobb brothers leave at 7:30 a.m. for their job after convincing Sally to stay home.

"I'm still gonna get some of that money you're getting. I went with you once, and that should count. Besides, I need some new clothes. I'm tired of always wearing these bib overalls, and I need new boots or shoes," Sally said as the brothers left.

"We'll watch all day, and if nothing different happens, I'm calling the boss. If the boss says the job is done, then we can get paid," Tommy explained to his brothers.

After watching all day, Tommy called the boss and explained that the second week of watching was the same as the first one, except for the hay delivery this Monday.

"What's our next step?"

The boss carefully explained the details of the next part of the job, and everything required of them.

"Okay, boss, we will start the job tomorrow at 3 p.m. when the lady leaves."

"Make sure you have everything planned, so there isn't a mistake. This job is important, and you will only have one opportunity to complete this job," the boss explained. "You have to get it right the first time."

"Yes, sir. You can count on us. We will follow all your instructions."

After hanging up the phone, Tommy explained everything to his brothers.

They go back home and tell Sally they are ready to finish the job, and she needs to help if she wants a share of the money.

"What do you expect me to do? I'm not strong like you guys. What can I do?"

"You'll have to borrow the pickup truck from your boyfriend."

"He's not my boyfriend. I just see him once in a while."

"Alright, I don't care what you call him. Just get his truck for tomorrow and make sure it has enough gas. We need it. I'll explain what you have to do later. Right now, we have to check the weather to make sure it isn't going to be raining," Tommy said.

"What difference does it make if it's raining or not? We've gotten wet before," Doug asks.

"If it's raining, we'll leave footprints and tire marks that the cops can use to find us. That is not going to happen," Tommy said with authority. "Also, make sure you all have gloves. I don't want you leaving any fingerprints for the cops."

The four spend hours working on their plan. Everyone gives their opinion on how to complete the project. They decide everything is ready, and the group is prepared for all possible events.

"Okay, you all have your jobs to do. Now get to bed. I still have some things to do before I can sleep. Tomorrow is gonna be a big day, and I want all of you ready," Tommy said.

"I'm too excited to sleep. I just want to get started so we can get that money." Steve said.

"Everyone, just be quiet and go to sleep. We have a lot of work to do tomorrow."

Chapter 11

David Drake orders a manufactured home to be placed seventy-five yards behind his 5,000-square-foot red brick ranch home and next to the bunkhouse and a shed, which is a replica of the main house. His wife, Paula, has spent the last year begging him to build a house for her mother so she can be close.

He has been putting off getting his mother-in-law a place since he doesn't like her and doesn't want to spend his money on her. Drake knows she doesn't like him. She just wants to aggravate him by staying close to her daughter.

To get his wife and mother-in-law off his back, he eventually purchased a Your Home Manufacturing building since they were the least expensive compared to other builders.

All the builders wanted their money before building, delivering, and setting up the house. Drake didn't like the requirement of paying first, but he didn't have a choice. All the other manufacturing companies had the same terms.

Finally, the building is delivered and placed behind the house. The workers put the house together and made it ready for occupancy.

His mother-in-law, Mary, settled into her new home. She immediately starts complaining and making a list of the things that need fixing.

"You are never happy," Drake tells Mary.

"David, look, the crown molding isn't complete. All the light switches are crooked. You can't completely open the refrigerator door because it's too close to the cabinets, and the front door doesn't close properly. There is also a long list of annoying things that need correcting. You have to get someone out here and fix this," Paula said, standing with her arm around her mother.

"Okay. Okay. I will call the company and get this fixed. Just get off my back."

It took several phone calls to the service department of Your Home Manufacturing before Drake received a call from the contractor.

"Hello. Mr. Drake, my name is Barry Herron with Your Home Manufacturing. I will be out there Monday at 9 a.m. to fix all your problems."

The next day, at 6 a.m. Herron texts that his van broke down and won't be there today. He will call on Wednesday and tell him when he can be there to fix the problems. By Wednesday evening, there still wasn't any word from Herron. Drake texts him and asks when he will be here. He doesn't get a response.

Finally, Herron arrived two days later. The man is five-foot-ten-inches tall, balding, and a bit on the chubby side. He is wearing a khaki work shirt and pants with dirty boots. He completed the crown molding and agreed to return the next day. Messages go back and forth between Herron and Drake for months, but the other work is never started or completed.

Frustrated, Drake deals with Herron's continued excuses and delays for almost a year. Drake calls Herron's boss to no avail. His excuses ranged from not completing a previous job to not having the materials to do the job and sending pictures of the bug bites on his stomach that he received while working under a house. According to his text, the bug bites put Herron in the hospital for intravenous antibiotics so that he couldn't work today.

The warranty on the house is about to expire. Herron assures

Drake that somebody will fix the problems since they have a record of the issues before the warranty expires.

At his wit's end, Drake decides to try another technique to get Barry Herron to his house. He offers the contractor $500 to come out and at least fix the light switches, which will keep his mother-in-law happy for a while.

"I'll be there in thirty minutes," Herron texts.

Drake prepares for the arrival and wonders if he will arrive this time.

Precisely thirty minutes later, Herron drives his dirty white panel van to the side of the house and meets Drake.

"Do you have the money for me?" Herron asks.

"Sure, it's over here in the shed. Follow me."

As the men enter the large 10 x 12 brick storage building, Drake picks up a shovel and hits Herron in the head with all his strength, knocking him to the ground.

"This has been going on for too long. I'm tired of your excuses. No one takes advantage of me," Drake said as he swings the shovel repeatedly.

Herron is lying face down. Drake hits him again, releasing all his frustration from the last eleven months.

"Now that I've gotten rid of this problem, I can get a reliable contractor to finish the house," he said to no one.

Later, he gets two of his trusted ranch hands, Bowman and Hurtz, to bury the body somewhere on his 550 acres and get rid of the truck. He tells his men to wear gloves and leave the van at an old, out-of-town hotel parking lot.

Herron's boss calls Drake several days later to inquire about his employee.

"He was supposed to be here, but like in the past, he never showed. Sorry, I don't know the location of Barry Herron," Drake said, honestly.

Chapter 12

First thing in the morning, Tommy quickly dresses in his bib overalls and prepares his vehicle for the big day's events. First, he gets the hidden money he received for recently cutting Frank Green's pasture. Then, Tommy takes his truck to the local mechanic to install a trailer hitch and wiring for the trailer and brake lights. He also purchases fuel for his vehicle and two-way radios for the job.

"Let's get to our spot at about 2 p.m. to make sure everything is going smoothly and there aren't any changes," Tommy said. "Sally, did you get your boyfriend's truck and fill it with gas?"

"Sure, I've done everything you told me, but I didn't have to get gas. The truck had a full tank. I'm ready to get started."

Doug rides with Sally, and Steve rides shotgun with Tommy. They patiently wait in their trucks and watch with binoculars until the lady leaves at 3 p.m.

"Okay, let's go. You know what to do," Tommy said over the two-way radio.

Both trucks travel to the Double H Boarding Ranch. Tommy backs his vehicle down the driveway and opens the gate with the automatic button on the keypad. Then he goes to the first horse trailer while Steve gets one of the two horses to put into the trailer. After the trailer is loaded and the two horses secured, Tommy drives out of Romeo to a predetermined location a few miles away, drops the trailer, and returns to the barn for the second trailer and two more horses.

Sally has backed up to the barn door. Doug and Sally quickly take the saddles, blankets, and equipment from the tack room and put everything of value in the bed of her truck. They leave and go to the secluded location.

Tommy and Steve removed all the horses and drove to the predetermined location. Two large, tall men are waiting for them.

"Looks like you got everything. The boss will be happy with the job you kids did," one of the men said. "Leave everything and get out of here. Remember to keep your mouths shut. We will dispose of the horses and trailers. You keep all the horse tack and sell it for your payment."

"Wait, the boss said we would get a lot of money for this job. He didn't say anything about us selling the tack," Tommy said.

"That's okay. If you don't want to sell the equipment, just leave it. We'll take it, but the tack is the only payment the boss is giving you."

"Oh, no. All that work, and we still have to sell everything to get any money," Doug said, slapping his forehead with the palm of his hand.

"What are you going to do with the horses?" Tommy asks.

"We will take them to the Tampa airport, get a flight, and take them to a slaughterhouse. Now, get going. We have a lot of work to do, and you're just in the way."

Disappointed, the Cobb children leave and go home.

"Did you know they were going to kill those horses?"

"Of course not, Sally. I wouldn't have done this if I knew they would kill the horses. You know I like all animals, especially horses," Tommy said after they arrived home.

"I thought you had this job all set. Now, we have to go to the farmer's market to sell this stuff to get any money. How could you be so stupid?" Sally asks.

"Don't worry. We can sell the tack at that big flea market called the Waldo Farmers and Flea Market. Nobody knows us there. It'll be okay. Trust me," Tommy said.

"Haven't we trusted you enough, and look what it got us. Just more work before we can get any money," Steve said.

"Will you quit complaining? We just have to sell the tack, and we'll have plenty of money."

"I hope you're right this time," Sally said.

Chapter 13

Nancy Jennings texts Steele that she will be there on Dec. 23rd. He responds that he has reservations for her at the Comfort Inn & Suites just a block off Williams Street in Dunnellon and will meet her at 4 p.m.

Nancy is waiting in the hotel lobby when Steele arrives. They embrace and kiss.

"Oh, Grant, it has been two long months since I last saw you. I've missed you."

"I know, Nancy, I feel the same. I'm glad you were able to visit."

"I have a lot of vacation time and decided to use it this week with you."

"Let's catch up over dinner. I hope you're ready to eat?"

"Yes, I'm starving. I skipped lunch today."

They talk and enjoy a leisurely dinner. Then, drive a few miles to a large retirement community, passing acres of rolling land with gentle hills and valleys.

Nancy sees numerous colorful twinkling lights on many elaborately decorated houses in the area.

"Some houses have different blow-up characters, mechanical reindeer, and nativity scenes. It is so beautiful. I'm also enjoying the horses playing in the fields."

"Now, we are going to the World Equestrian Center to see their Christmas light display. This place is unbelievable," Steele said.

"I didn't know you were interested in horses."

"I'm only learning about them because we have a serial killer knocking off jockeys."

"I can't believe it. Are you trying to find another serial killer? Wasn't the one in the Villages enough for you?"

"Of course, it was, but I don't like killers, and I can't just ignore a person or persons killing innocent jockeys," Steele said as he drove to WEC.

"I'm sure you will find the culprit as you did in the Villages. Now, let's enjoy our ride and not talk about work," Nancy said as they arrived at WEC a few minutes later.

They enjoy the cool weather as they walk hand-in-hand, and Steele gives her a coin.

"What is this? It looks like clouds on it?" she asks, putting the coin in her pocket.

"It is a coin representing the Bit of Heaven Thoroughbred Farms. All the big ranches have something like it. It's like their business card, only it is a coin. Some ranch hands solder the coin on their large belt buckles to show where they work."

"Thank you. I will keep it as a memento of my first time in the horse country."

They continued walking through the winter wonderland of the traditional regalia of the season with larger-than-life ornaments and a Christmas tree maze.

"Oh, Grant. You're right. All the colorful trees and twinkling lights are festive, putting me in the Christmas spirit. Everywhere I look, there are more vibrant and multi-colored lights. I feel like a kid on Christmas morning."

"I'm glad you are enjoying yourself."

After walking through the Christmas tree maze, they decided to have a drink in the Yellow Pony Pub and Garden in the WEC hotel, decorated with red and white poinsettias everywhere.

"I'm curious. Why did you make reservations for me at the hotel? Why couldn't I stay at your place?

"When I moved here, the only place I could find and afford to rent was a small studio apartment in Dunnellon. It is barely big enough for me, let alone two of us. I will show you my place before you leave," Steele said as he drove her back to her hotel.

"Would you like to come in and have a drink? I know you like Jack Daniels, and I brought a bottle. Then maybe you could spend the night and have breakfast here."

"That would be a perfect ending for this day. I have off this week, but I'm still on call," Steele said.

They enjoy the evening. The next day, in the late afternoon, the sheriff's office calls Steele about a robbery.

"Sorry, I have to go to work. I will pick you up for dinner," Steele said.

"That will be fine. I can do a lot of work on my computer while you are gone. I'll be ready for dinner when you call," Nancy said.

Chapter 14

On Christmas Eve, Helen Lane, owner of the Double H Boarding Ranch, returns home to discover all the horses are gone. Shocked, she calls the sheriff's office and informs them that someone has stolen all her horses. Steele drives to the boarding ranch with blue lights and sirens to investigate.

"I'm Detective Grant Steele with the sheriff's office," as he shows his badge and I.D.

"My name is Helen Lane, and my husband Howard and I own this ranch. I came home from town and saw the barn door open, and all the horses were gone, and that's when I called the cops. I'm devastated. Why would anyone steal all the horses, especially on Christmas Eve?"

Steele uses his radio to request CSI Wagner to join him. Walking into the barn, he notices the strong smell of pine shavings, oiled leather, and horse poop from the stalls.

"Mrs. Lane, how many horses are missing?"

"We board six horses. Their saddles, bridles, and blankets are gone too. They must have taken the horses in the owner's horse trailers that we kept on the side of the barn."

"So, the missing horses don't belong to you and your husband?"

"No, boarding horses is our business, and now everything is gone," she said with tears running down her cheek.

Steele hands her a handkerchief.

"Is your husband home? Can I talk to him?"

"Yes, he's home, but I don't think he will talk to you. I have a helper come in each day for three hours to care for him while I do my chores in town because he has dementia and gets confused easily, especially in the evening."

"I'm sure we won't have to disturb him tonight."

CSI Wagner arrives and walks around the barn using a high-powered flashlight to look for footprints or tire marks. He notices three areas with tall yellowing grass next to the barn where Mrs. Lane kept the horse trailers.

"It is too dark to see clearly, but I didn't find any evidence to tell us the perp's identity. The tack room is empty. The perp took everything that's not nailed down," Wagner said. "I'll start getting fingerprints from the stalls, and maybe we'll get lucky."

"Mrs. Lane, what time did you leave, and when did you return?" Steele asks.

"I always leave about 3 p.m. after putting the horses in their stalls. I usually go grocery shopping, do chores, and return at about 6 p.m. every day except Sunday. I don't leave the ranch on Sundays. That is the day the owners normally brush, groom, and spend time with their horses. Sunday is when they usually take their horse for a ride," she said.

"That only gives the perps three hours to remove everything. There had to be more than one perp to accomplish this in that amount of time," Wagner said.

"Okay, Mrs. Lane, we will look around some more, and Wagner will collect fingerprints. The report will be ready in a few days. You can pick up a copy and send it to your insurance company."

"We don't have any insurance. It was too expensive, and we were just getting by with the money from boarding horses. There was a time when we had plenty of money, but we had a spell of bad luck with the stock market. We lost two of our borders, and the cost of feed and supplies kept increasing, and now we can barely manage. What a horrible way to spend Christmas. Why would anyone do something like this?" Mrs. Lane asks.

Parker enters the barn and looks around.

"Hi, I'm Ashley Parker from the *Ocala Star Banner*, and I have some questions for you. I heard you tell the detective that you didn't have insurance. Is that correct?"

"We originally had insurance, but it was too expensive, and we couldn't afford the premiums, so we had to drop it. We also lost two boarders and had to choose between insurance, feed, and hay for the animals."

Parker continues talking to Helen Lane and gets the information about the robbery.

Parker's story of the theft and how the Lanes didn't have insurance is on the paper's second page the next day. Her story evokes compassion from the general public and the horse community, and they send money to the newspaper for the Lanes.

After collecting the money for a month Parker gives the funds to Mrs. Lane, and she uses the money to buy feed and hay and puts an ad in the paper looking for new customers. The ad was successful and brought in new boarders for her.

Chapter 15

After spending a night at his home, Steele goes to the hotel to pick up Nancy for dinner.

"Where are we going to dinner? Everything is closed on Christmas day," Nancy asks.

"We are going to the Chinese restaurant in Ocala. They're always open on Christmas and New Year's Day."

"I like Chinese food. That would be great."

As they enter the oriental restaurant, Steele touches his overcoat pocket, feels the small box and smiles. The large room has black, red, and gold themes with large Chinese-painted wall fans on dark red walls and paper lanterns hanging from the ceiling.

An elderly Chinese woman escorts them to a booth and gives them plates for the buffet. They decide on hot tea. The woman brings two classical blue and white ceramic cups without handles and a matching teapot to their table while they fill their plates with food.

"Here, try some of this moo shu beef. It is delicious," Steele said, giving Nancy a forkful of food.

"Mmm. It is good."

After several visits to the buffet, they are content and relaxing with tea and a fortune cookie.

"What does your fortune say? Mine says this is my lucky day."

Steele takes Nancy's hand across the table.

"Nancy, we have been dating for about two years, and I think it is time to take it to the next level. Before I met you, I was engaged to someone for two years before she cheated on me. I was devastated and didn't think I would ever trust again until I met you. I love you and have loved you for a long time. Will you give me the honor of marrying me?" He takes the small black velvet box from his overcoat pocket and opens it for Nancy. She sees a Neil Lane designer engagement ring.

"Oh, Grant. Yes. Yes. I will marry you. I love you, too. My fortune cookie was right. Today is my lucky day," Nancy said.

Steele takes the ring out of the box and slips it on her finger.

"It is so beautiful. I never expected you to propose. It's like a rainbow of color sparkling on my hand," Nancy said as she held out her hand, admiring the ring.

"I have a lot to tell you about my past. I feel you should know so you can change your mind. I have been going to anger management sessions because I almost killed a guy when I worked in Los Angeles. The guy was molesting a child, and I just snapped. I don't like pedophiles." Steele said.

"It's alright. I learned about that when someone stole your laptop in the Villages, and I had to check it for malware. Remember?"

"You knew all this time and didn't say anything?" Steele asks.

"Yes, I gave the captain my word that I wouldn't tell anyone what I found on your laptop," she said. "And my answer stays the same. Yes, I will marry you."

"Wonderful. Oh, look who just came into the restaurant."

"Hi. This Chinese restaurant is the only place that appears to be open today, so, naturally, we would meet," Wagner said as he spotted the couple. "How are you doing, Nancy?"

"Oh, Wagner, it is great to see you. Look at my Christmas present from Grant," she said, showing the ring on her left hand.

"Congratulations, Steele, and good luck to you, Nancy. The ring is unexpected. Why didn't you tell me, Steele?"

"I wanted it to be a surprise. I didn't tell anyone."

"How long will you be in town, Nancy?" Wagner asks.

"I'll be in town until we celebrate the 2024 New Year. Then, I must return to work. But Grant and I have to talk about our future after my big surprise," Nancy said.

"Well, I guess I'll sit at the other end of the restaurant and let you two be alone. I didn't want to spoil your special moment," Wagner said.

"No, stay, and let's talk. Nancy and I will have a lot of time to talk before she leaves," Grant says happily.

"It will be nice to catch up and not have to eat alone on Christmas day."

Steele moves to Nancy's side of the booth, puts his arm around her, and Wagner sits across from them. The older waitress gives Wagner a plate and brings him a blue and white ceramic cup without handles and a fresh pot of tea.

Chapter 16

The Cobb children are hanging out in their old single-wide trailer with the metal roof oozing rust, and the siding buckling, allowing the wind to blow their shabby curtains around. They live in the Romeo area, just north of Dunnellon. The houses are few and far apart, and the Cobb's closest neighbor is less than a quarter mile away. The kids sit on the floor, complaining about how the boss ripped them off. They all jump when someone pounds on their aluminum door since they have few visitors. Tommy answers and sees his mother.

"Mom, where have you been? We haven't seen you in years. What are you doing here?"

An older woman, about five-foot-four-inches and very thin, wearing a faded house dress and old loafers without socks, enters the house carrying a plastic garbage bag filled with her clothes. Her short white hair makes her wrinkled face look gray and drab.

The front room is bare except for an old sofa and a metal floor lamp with a dirty shade in the corner. The boys are all sitting on the worn linoleum floor, leaning against the couch, and Sally sits on one of the four plastic-covered stools by the kitchen counter.

"Well, you know I was an alcoholic before I left. I had a hard time getting clean. I hit bottom before I found an excellent mission in Gainesville that has helped for the past year. I've been sober for eleven months and decided I was ready to come home and take care of you kids," Jill Cobb said.

"Well, you could have stayed away. Maybe we aren't ready for you to come home. Because of you, we've had Social Services checking on us, telling us what to do, and saying they would put us into foster care if we didn't behave," Sally said.

"I came back to take care of you and tell you how sorry I am. I will go to Alcoholics Anonymous meetings every week. I'm willing to try to make this up to you. I just want to be a good mom for you," she said.

"Why weren't you a good mother when we needed you? You could have stopped Dad from beating on us. But no, you were always drunk, or you didn't care. That's when we needed you to help us. But you left us. We're doing okay without you, and we don't need you now," Doug said.

"Let's give Mom a chance. If she stays here, maybe the social services lady will leave us alone," Tommy said.

"All I'm asking for is a chance. Let me show you how much I love you. Now, I'll start cleaning up this place to prove I want to help you. How did you kids manage to get everything so dirty?" she said as she entered the small kitchen and attacked the pile of dirty dishes.

There was another knock at the door. Hesitantly, Tommy opens the door to a large, middle-aged woman from the children and families department of social services. The woman is wearing her jet-black hair in a bun at the nape of her neck. Her brown pantsuit is bulging at the buttons and is worn but clean, and she is carrying a tattered briefcase as she enters the trailer.

"I know I haven't been here in a while, but the mission notified us that your mother was coming home. I came to check on everyone," the lady said as she wrote on her clipboard. "Mrs. Cobb, my name is Beverly Thorne, and I've been your children's social worker for a couple of years."

"Why are you bothering my children? Sally is nineteen, Tommy is eighteen, Steve is seventeen, and Doug is the only minor at sixteen," Mrs. Cobb asks.

"We had to keep checking on the children because, under the law, Steve and Doug are considered minors. As you can see, they are all underweight, but they are clean. We had to be sure the older children cared for the younger ones. So far, they have been doing a good job, so we allowed them to stay together with monthly check-ups. We don't like to split up families. And now that you are back, are you planning to get a job to support them, or do you expect the local churches and charities to continue clothing, feeding, and caring for them?" she asks.

"Of course, I plan to get a job as a waitress," Mrs. Cobb said.

"I hope you find work in a place that doesn't sell liquor," the social worker said.

"I know I'm an alcoholic. I can't be around liquor, so I'm not tempted, but I'll find a good job."

"That is excellent, Mrs. Cobb. Be advised I will be checking on your employment and will come to the house every month to see how you and the children are doing," the social worker said as she left.

After a few minutes of silence, the children start talking to their mother. They have so many questions.

"Where are you going to get a job?" they ask in unison.

"I interviewed for a job at the Go for Donuts restaurant in Dunnellon before I came here. They will let me know tomorrow when I go there," the mother said.

The children had asked numerous questions, and their mother answered them.

"I've always wondered what happened to Dad. Do you know where he went?" Sally finally asks.

"How would I know what happened to that man? I was always drunk and didn't know what he was doing, and I didn't care."

"He left just after you did and didn't take his truck."

"I can't believe he left his truck. I think he loved the truck more than any of us. He spent all his money and time washing and waxing it. He spent a lot of our money competing in truck and car shows too."

"Did you have a problem with him and tell him to leave?" Sally asks.

"Okay, let's stop talking about your dad. I don't even want to think about him anymore. Why don't you tell me what you have been doing since I've been gone?" Jill Cobb asks.

"We aren't doing anything. Why are you asking? Are you going to stay with us now?"

"How will I care for you if I don't stay here?"

"We don't have an empty bed. When you and Dad left, we each got a bed, and Doug got a cot," Tommy said.

"Don't worry. I'll sleep on the old couch. I don't want to take your bed. Now that's settled, let me get back to the dishes."

The children cautiously accept that their mother is sober and wonder if she will leave them again. As Jill cleans the kitchen, the children scatter through the house to their rooms.

"Good thing we sold all that horse tack before she got here. Did you hide the money?" Doug whispers to Tommy in their bedroom.

"Of course, I did. Do you think I'm stupid or something? Keep your voice down and stop talking about the money. We can talk about it after she leaves for work tomorrow."

"I want to buy some new clothes and maybe some boots," Sally said after walking into Tommy's room and heard him whisper to Doug.

"Are you crazy? We can't do anything with the money now. Everyone would notice new clothes and ask us where we got them. Right now, we have to lay low. Do you understand?" Tommy asks.

"How long do I have to wait to get some boots?" Sally asks.

"Right now, everyone is looking at us, and with Mom here, we can't do anything to show we have any money. So just be quiet about it. Okay?"

"Well, I don't have a choice, but I want to get new boots as soon as possible."

"What's the hurry? You've worn those shoes for a while. Can't you wait till everything cools down?"

"I guess I don't have a choice since you're the one holding the money."

"That's right, and don't forget it."

Chapter 17

After the New Year's celebration, Nancy returns home with a promise to return for another visit soon. Steele and Wagner focus on their serial killer and all the horses someone has stolen. As they drive out to the ranches, the dispatcher notifies them of an abandoned vehicle at a mom and pop motel in the rundown area of Ocala.

"Okay. We are almost there," Steele uses the radio to tell the dispatcher as they arrive.

"I'm Detective Grant Steele, and this is CSI Jack Wagner. We understand you called in an abandoned vehicle," he said while showing his badge and I.D. to the tired old manager of the neglected motel.

"That white van has been in our parking lot and has not moved in over a week," the manager said.

"Did you look inside? Is the door locked?"

"I didn't touch anything. I don't want to find a dead body or drugs or something. That's why I called the cops."

With his gun drawn, Steele walked to the vehicle and carefully opened the driver's door. After he looked inside, he holstered his weapon and opened the sliding panel on the driver's side of the van.

"Everything looks okay. There isn't a dead body, just a bunch of building materials and tools. Wagner will dust it for prints, and I'll call in the plate to find its owner."

The truck's owner is Your Home Manufacturing, and Steele gets their phone number and address. He went to their office and discovered that Barry Herron was assigned the vehicle to do contracting work for them.

"I haven't heard from Herron in about a week. He's not my most reliable worker, but he does good work when he actually shows up," Herron's boss said. "I already called David Drake because that was Herron's last job. He said Barry wasn't there either."

"Is Herron a gambler, have enemies, or does he owe anyone money?" Steele asks.

"No, he didn't gamble, but he does have a history of drinking binges. He would go off and drink for a few days and show up for work after he recovered from his hangover."

"How often does this happen?" Steele asks.

"He goes on drinking binges on a regular basis, Herron isn't very dependable, but he does good work for me when he isn't drunk."

"We'll put a BOLO out on Herron as a missing person, and please call us if he shows up," Steele said, giving him his business card.

"Something may have happened to him because he's never been gone this long. Normally, he would've checked in by now, but if I hear from him, I'll call you," Herron's boss said.

Steele returned to the scene as Wagner finished getting evidence off the vehicle.

"I couldn't find any good prints. They are all smudged. So, the perp must have worn gloves and smeared any prints in the vehicle. I did notice that someone pushed the driver's seat back for a very tall person to drive the truck. We need to find out how tall Herron is," Wagner said.

The car gets towed to the Your Home Manufacturing location, and Steele and Wagner drive to Drake's ranch.

"Sorry to bother you, but we have a few questions."

"No problem, Detective. What can I do for you?" Drake asks.

"We understand Barry Herron worked on your manufacturing

home in your backyard."

"That is true when he bothered to show up," Drake said.

"What do you mean when he bothered to show up?"

"He always said he would be here and give me a time and day. I would wait all day for him, but he always had an excuse to cancel just before he was to arrive.

"When was the last time he was here?" Steele asks.

"I don't remember exactly what day it was, but I think it was a couple of months ago," Drake said.

"Can you tell me how tall Herron is?"

"He was about five-foot-ten-inches. He's of average height and a little on the heavy side. Why do you ask?"

"We just need it for our report. Okay, if you hear from Herron, call me," Steele said, giving him his business card.

"Okay, but I doubt he will call now after not hearing from him for so long."

"It seems strange that no one reported him missing. You think his family would wonder where he was," Wagner said as they walked to their car. "And it is apparent that a very tall man drove the car since the driver's seat was moved back.

They enjoy watching the horses running and playing in the fields while driving to Moore's ranch.

"Hello, Mr. Moore. Have you heard about the stolen horses and jockeys?"

"I've heard about the three dead jockeys, but I didn't know about the missing horses."

"Somebody robbed Helen Lane's boarding ranch on Christmas Eve. The robbers took six horses and everything of value. Do you know who would do something like that?" Steele asks.

"They are friendly people, and everyone liked them. Mrs. Lane had many financial problems, caring for her husband and running the boarding stable alone, but I never heard her complain."

"Thank you for your time, Mr. Moore. If you think of anything that could help us, please call," Steele said as they left.

"I guess we should check on Green before heading back."

Green's house is dark, and no one answers the door. They decide to check out the home in the historic district to see if Green's vehicle is there. The historic house is also dark, and no cars are in the driveway or parked on the street. Disappointed, they left.

Chapter 18

On a Saturday at the end of January, a Robin Egg Blue 2002 Toyota Camry traveled north on Highway 41 and drove into the Romeo area. The older vehicle has two women and two men passengers, but they aren't related to each other.

The driver continued until he found a dirt road. He turned onto the road and drove until a dead-end sign stopped him.

"Okay, we're here," said the driver, a short man wearing tall boots, heavy pants, a warm jacket, and a floppy hat. All four of them are wearing bird-watching clothes. They all have binoculars around their necks and hold a small notebook with a brochure showing pictures of different birds.

"We should be able to observe the red-cockaded woodpeckers. They have been on the endangered list since 1970, but I have it on good authority that we can find those birds in this area. Keep your eyes open," Wally Squire, Morriston's bird-watching group leader, said with authority. He holds a demeaning regular job and enjoys the power of self-appointing himself as the group's leader.

The amateur bird watchers excitedly leave the car and start walking in all directions, looking for the woodpecker. They wander around, looking through their binoculars.

"Look. There in the tree is a Florida scrub jay. Check our guide. I think they are also declining," one of the ladies said.

"Has anyone found any other birds to add to our list?" Emily

Mayer, a bird watcher, asks.

"Okay, everyone, you know, you have to be quiet, so we don't scare the birds away," Squire said.

The group roams around for several hours in all directions. Suddenly, they hear a high-pitched shriek. They scramble through tall trees and bushes until they find Emily Mayer lying in soft dirt and screaming for someone to help her.

"Here, let me help you," Squires said as he tugs on Emily's arm, pulling her into a standing position.

"I... I touched a hand. See for yourself, Emily said as she brushed the dirt off her clothes.

Everyone was looking at the sinking soft earth. They see something that resembles a hand.

"That isn't a hand. It's a branch that looks like a hand," Squires said.

"No. You're wrong. Look again. It's a hand. Someone call 9-1-1 and get the cops out here," the other man said.

The bird watchers are all trying to call the cops when the screams and commotion bring Sally and Tommy to the area. A couple of neighbors also arrive to see what all the fuss is about.

"What are you doing on my land?" Tommy asks with a shotgun in his hands.

The neighbors see Tommy's shotgun and hear the police siren. They don't want trouble and return to their homes less than a quarter mile away.

"We didn't know we were trespassing. We didn't see any 'No Trespassing' signs. We're bird watchers. We're looking for the red-cockaded woodpeckers," Squires said. "We don't want any trouble."

Everyone starts talking simultaneously about the hand in the soft dirt and that the cops are on the way.

"Why did you call the cops? Sally asks.

Before she received an answer, Detective Steele arrived with the blue lights sweeping the area and the noisy siren shutting down to a moan. He notices all the people crowding around an area of land with tall trees and bushes but no other houses except an old trailer hidden in tall grass.

"What is going on here? We have reports of a dead body. Who is responsible for this call?" Steele asks.

"It looks like somebody buried a body in this soft ground that looks like a shallow grave," Squires proudly points to the slumped soil softer than the surrounding area.

After checking the area, Steele sees the skeletal hand. He uses his radio to request Wagner and the coroner's bus. Tommy took this opportunity to return the shotgun to the house.

"I don't need this aggravation," Steele mumbles, reminding himself to stop his bad habit.

While waiting for Wagner, Steele questions the birdwatchers and learns that Tommy and Sally live in the nearby trailer. Eventually, Jill follows Steve and Doug outside to see what the commotion is all about.

"What is going on? Why are you all on my land?" Jill asks.

"What is your name, and why are you out here?" Steele asks.

"I'm Jill Cobb, and this is my land and my children.

By the time Wagner arrives on the scene, the birdwatchers have given their names and addresses to Steele. They each told stories of their actions until they found the hand sticking out of the ground and called the police.

Ashley Parker arrived and stood in the background, observing everyone.

"Exactly where does your land end? Is the grave on your land?"

"What are you talking about, a grave?" Jill asks.

"It seems the birdwatchers have discovered a grave."

Wagner starts removing the dirt around the extended arm and hand.

"Looks like you found another body," Wagner said as he

brushed away the soft dirt.

When the coroner's assistant arrived, Wagner had a large portion of a skeleton above the shallow grave. He is ready to help the coroner's assistant put what's left of the body in a body bag.

"Hey, Steele. You need to see this. There appear to be two bodies in this grave. The medical examiner will have a field day with this."

"How long will it take to get any information on the remains?" Steele asked the assistant.

"I don't know. The medical examiner will have to give you that information. I've never even seen anything like this before."

With help from Wagner, the M.E.'s assistant puts each skeleton into a body bag.

"Hey, Steele, could you get me the large evidence boxes out of the back of my car? I need to get a lot of this dirt back to the lab."

"Sure, why do you need to take this dirt back?"

"Because the dirt will have evidence, and hopefully, I will find pieces of their clothes," Wagner said. "Also, see if the people in the trailer have a shovel."

Steele returned holding a wood handle shovel with a flat blade.

"That is great. With the flat blade, I can shovel the dirt without cutting into any evidence still in the grave."

Steele leaves, and Wagner continues working on the grave. Parker has already interviewed the birdwatchers and the Cobb family and asked Wagner questions before he left. She then left to write her story about birdwatchers falling into a shallow grave and discovering two skeletons.

"This is a really great story," she said to no one.

Chapter 19

Erin Kelly, a former roommate, emails Ashley Parker and asks if she can visit for a few days. When she arrives, the two go out to the Go for Donuts restaurant in Dunnellon for lunch.

"You changed your hairstyle," Parker asks as she eats an egg salad sandwich oozing down her hand.

"I was tired of the long hair, and this Pixie cut is so easy to style."

"It looks great. And I like the light brown hair color too. So, tell me, what are you doing now?"

"I've been looking for employment, but no one will hire me in The Villages. I'm trying to live on my unemployment benefits now, but it's tough. When the FBI arrested the owners of the Cosmopolitan Hotel, they closed the hotel, and I lost my job. Also, since our lease on our apartment ended on December 31, I have been renting monthly. If you're willing, I hope to find a job here and maybe share an apartment with you again."

"That would be great. We always had a great time while we shared an apartment, even in college."

"Good. By the way, how is your job going?"

"My job at the Ocala paper is excellent, and I'm also making more money than I did at the Village Chronicle. Why don't we start looking for a two-bedroom apartment today? After we find a place to live, I will take you job hunting in Ocala."

"That would be great, Ashley. I was hoping you would say that."

After lunch, they go to the apartment manager's office and find a furnished place to live in Dunnellon, and Ashley gets out of her current lease.

"Now, I just need to find a job, and I'll return to the Villages and pack my things. I'm so excited to be living with you again, Ashley."

"We did have fun living together, didn't we? Maybe you can uncover another great story for me as you did in The Villages last year."

After visiting several hotels in the Ocala area, Erin interviews at the over one-hundred-year-old historic five-star hotel downtown, at the Ocala Manor, offering luxurious accommodations. She enters the six-floor hotel and notices the rich, dark paneling with a long line of brass and Swarovski crystal chandeliers hanging from the ceiling in the lobby and long hall. After a brief interview, Erin was offered a hotel guest services representative job and asked to begin employment on February 2.

"They want to train me before the Valentine's Day rush begins. I'm so excited to have a job again," Erin says.

"Congrats. It's wonderful that you found a job and now we have an apartment. Life is good."

"I'm going back and packing all my things. I can be back by February 1, so I don't have to pay for another month's rent."

"Great. That will give me time to clear out my old apartment and move into the new one," Parker said.

"Oh, I almost forgot to tell you. Do you remember Chuck Vaughn?"

"Sure, he worked at the Hands-On-Therapy shop when someone almost beat him to death. Why do you ask?"

"Well, my knee was giving me trouble again, and the doctor had me go back to get more therapy, and Chuck was my therapist. While talking, he asked about you. I told him I was visiting, and he wanted me to tell you he asked about you. Chuck also asked me for your address and phone number, which I gave him, but now the address will be different. I hope that was okay?"

"That was fine. You can give Chuck our new address when you go back. We became good friends while he was in the hospital and while I took him to his therapy. It will be nice to hear from him again. Is your knee doing better after the therapy?"

"It's all good now. I guess I just needed a bit more stretching exercises and massage."

A few days later, Erin settled into the apartment with Ashley and began her new job wearing a white shirt with the hotel emblem, black slacks, and the hotel staff name tag. She is eager to learn all the hotel procedures. While exploring the hotel, Erin meets the manager and some of the housekeeping staff. Eventually, she discovers that certain parts of the hotel are locked, and the keys she received don't open all the doors, including the basement. The locked doors have a sign 'For Employees Only,' but her keys won't open them. Erin tries talking to one of the housekeeping ladies about the locked doors, but she doesn't speak English and avoids Erin. She eventually learns that the day manager is fluent in Spanish, and she and Maria are the only ones who can communicate with the ladies.

The manager told Erin to block several rooms on the first floor. If the hotel gets completely booked, she can ask the manager which blocked rooms could be available for guests.

Erin's curiosity is out of control, and she can't wait to tell Ashley about her discovery and discuss all the possibilities of why the doors are locked. She wonders why guests can't rent certain rooms until the hotel is full. Her imagination is going wild, and she can't wait until her shift ends so she can go home and talk to Ashley about this mystery.

Chapter 20

Wagner has been analyzing the dirt from the makeshift grave for two weeks. He notified Steele that he had found something interesting.

"The medical examiner told me the bodies were in the ground for about three years. He said both bodies were men of middle age. The first skeleton in the grave had evidence of being hit on the back of the head with a small round object. There wasn't any evidence of trauma with the second body. He also says that the second body may have died from natural causes since he hasn't found the cause of death yet, but he will continue to analyze the bones," Steele said.

"I discovered two pairs of cowboy boots at the bottom of the grave. There were also small fragments of cloth that contained cotton and polyester. I'm trying to get some DNA off the material and boots."

"How can boots and cloth still be intact after three years in the ground?" Steele asks.

"Because the tanning process of the boots changes the chemistry inside the leather fibers, making it more difficult for the enzymes from bacteria in the soil to break it down. Natural cotton usually disintegrates in about five months, but cotton with polyester can survive for many years."

"All I have to do now is look at all the missing person's reports for two middle-aged men reported missing three years ago."

After checking the missing person's reports in Marion County,

Steele also looked into the surrounding police departments and the online police records to no avail.

"I can't believe two men go missing, and no one reports them gone. The next step is to talk to the Cobb family since the grave was close to their trailer. Do you want to come along?"

"Sure. I need to get some fresh air after dealing with the dirt from the grave."

They arrive at the Cobb's trailer, and Tommy invites them in. Steele explains that the bodies found in the grave are on their property.

"That is not true. My property stops just before the grave," Jill Cobb said.

"We found that the two skeletons buried three years ago were middle-aged men. Strangely, no one reported them missing. Do you remember anything unusual happening about three years ago since you live so close to the grave?" Steele asks the family.

"No, I don't remember anything happening," Jill said.

"Wait, Dad left about three years ago," Sally said. "I remember because that's when the beatings stopped.

"What do you mean he left?" Steele asks.

"Dad left three years ago but didn't take his truck."

"None of you thought you should report him missing, especially since he didn't take his truck? The red Ford F250 truck with flames painted on the hood and a lot of chrome and dark tinted windows outside is your dad's?"

"Yeah. It's Dad's truck, and I've been using it since he left," Tommy said.

"We didn't want him to come back. So, we just waited every day to see if he would come back, and each day that passed, we were glad that he didn't show up," Steve said.

"What about you, Mrs. Cobb? Do you remember anything happening three years ago?"

"Why would she remember anything? She was always drunk

and hanging around with her boyfriend," Sally said.

"Can you give me the name of your boyfriend, Mrs. Cobb? We will need to talk to him."

Jill Cobb plops on the couch, puts her head in her hands, and starts crying.

"What is the matter, Mom? Are you okay?" Doug asks.

"I'm glad it's over. I can't bear this guilt anymore. Now that I'm sober, I can't live with this anymore."

"Mrs. Cobb, what do you mean? Can you explain further?"

"Johnny Nolan was my boyfriend, and he was always upset because he knew that my husband, Peter, would beat the kids and me. One day, Peter came outside looking for me and swearing the whole time while the kids were hiding from him in the house. Johnny happened to be there and picked up the shovel and hit him with the handle. Peter fell to the ground, and Johnny started digging a grave for him where he fell when Johnny had a heart attack or something.

He grabbed his chest and fell over before he could finish digging the grave. That is why the bodies weren't buried very deep. I checked, and Johnny wasn't breathing, so I rolled Peter in the grave and then Johnny. I covered the grave as best I could," Jill said. "I was drunk and upset because I loved Johnny, and he died trying to help me. Johnny didn't have a family, so there wasn't anyone to notify. After that, I couldn't stand being around Johnny's grave when I knew my husband was there too. So, I just left and got drunk."

"Stand up, Mrs. Cobb, put your hands behind you, and turn around. I'm arresting you for not reporting a death and burying both bodies."

Steele was upset hearing the story on how the men died. But he handcuffed Mrs. Cobb and read her the Miranda warning.

"You have the right to remain silent. Anything you say can be used against you in a court of law. You have the right to an attorney.

If you cannot afford an attorney, one will be appointed to you. Mrs. Cobb, do you understand your rights? As I've read them to you?"

"Sure, I understand them, but I don't have no money for a fancy lawyer."

"You will be appointed a lawyer if you can't afford one."

"You can't take her. She just got here a few days ago," Doug said.

"I'm sorry, but I'm arresting her for burying someone who died because of criminal activity. If she goes to trial and a jury convicts her, she will be guilty of a felony. That is punishable in county jail for one year or no more than five years. There could also be a fine between $1,000 and $5,000," Steele said to Tommy as he walked Mrs. Cobb out to his vehicle with Wagner following behind.

"This can't be happening. We don't have that kind of money to pay for a fine. " Now, the Social Services lady will be sticking her nose in our business again," Tommy said. "Maybe we can sell that old Saturn Mom drove here."

"Maybe I could keep the old car and get a job. Then I would have money for some real clothes. What do you think, Tommy?" Steve asks.

"That old car isn't worth anything, and if you use it to find a job, how will you pay for gas until you get your first paycheck?" Tommy asks. "Let's wait for a while before making any big decisions."

"Why can't I ever get anything? You always get your way," Steve said.

"Because I'm the head of the house."

Chapter 21

Steele goes to Wagner's office and asks him for some computer help.

"What do you need?"

"Can you check the computer to see if there is anything about stealing or kidnapping horses?"

"Sure. This shouldn't take long."

Minutes later, information on horse slaughter facts pops up from Wikipedia.

"I've got something about horses slaughtered. What do you want to know?"

"Is there actually a place that slaughters horses?" Steele asks.

They read that horses are transported to regulated plants in Mexico and Canada to be slaughtered. The largest horse meat-consuming countries were China, Russia, and Italy.

The courts outlawed horse meat in the United States for use in pet food in the 1970s.

"Can you believe pet food contained horse meat just fifty years ago?" Wagner said.

He continued to read that some European countries have traditionally eaten horse meat. Although United States horses have never been raised for human consumption, American horses have been bought, stolen, and slaughtered by a foreign-owned industry for sale in high-end restaurants in Europe and Asia. So, horse meat can satisfy diners' palates in countries such as France, Belgium,

Italy, and Japan. According to the California Livestock and Identification Bureau Statistics, the 1998 ban on slaughtering horses in California was followed by a thirty-four percent decrease in horse theft.

"According to the Director of the American Horse Protection Association, Stolen Horse International is one modern-day organization in the United States that still works to reconnect stolen horses with their owners. They also estimate that 40,000 horses per year are stolen in the U.S.," Wagner said.

"Wow. Do you think somebody sent all the stolen horses to the slaughter plants?" Steele asks.

"I can't think of another reason to take horses. You can't sell quarter horses without their paperwork, and thoroughbreds have their upper lip tattooed with a unique number to identify the horse and its owner," Wagner said.

"I didn't think horse stealing, especially for slaughter, was so rampant."

"It also shows that DOT has officers at enforcement points to ensure the proper transportation of horses, but it doesn't have any jurisdiction beyond transportation. It doesn't say why, but the slaughter plants won't accept horses that are severely lame or disabled."

"While you were looking up the info on horse slaughter, I checked the Florida Law Enforcement Handbook and found Florida statute 828.125 (a) shows it is a second-degree felony to commit aggravated abuse of a horse, with a minimum mandatory penalty of one year in state prison and a $3,500 fine."

"We need to find those horses," Wagner said.

"We should talk to the ranchers again. Maybe they know who's stealing the horses. It has to be a group of people because one person couldn't pull off a job this big," Steele said. "I'll check on other ranches farther away from the horse trail. Do you want to come along?"

"Sure, where are we going?"

"We will visit Frank Green, Howard Lane, David Drake, and Ed Moore to see if they own weapons or have any information about the stolen horses.

Steele and Wagner didn't get any answers about the missing horses from the ranchers. Then they stopped at the Black Dominoes ranch.

"Mr. Moore, have you learned anything about your missing horses?"

"Well, I did get a call asking for money for the two horses, but the quarter horses weren't worth the amount they were asking. So, I told them they could keep them," Moore said.

"Did you recognize the voice, or did the person say anything that would reveal who the caller was?"

"No, it could have been anyone."

They leave Moore's ranch and visit Four Seasons Ranch, owned by Peggy and Bob Hagan. Then, they went to Mark and Betty Cordell at the Rolling Hills Ranch. They are both located north of S.R. 40.

The Hagans knew nothing about the missing horses or how someone could have taken them.

Mark Cordell remembers that several quarter horses went missing years ago, but he can't recall the circumstances since it wasn't his horses involved.

Steele and Wagner thanked them for their time and returned to the office.

They also learned from the ranch hands that it is common practice for the ranchers to have a collection of handguns and rifles to kill predators like snakes, dogs, and coyotes found on their land.

Chapter 22

Frank Green decided to visit Morgan Eastman in Tallahassee. He goes to her office and asks to see her.

"I'm sorry, sir, but the Lt. Governor's schedule is full today. She has an opening at 3 p.m. tomorrow. Would you like to make an appointment with her?" the secretary asks.

"Just tell her that Frank Green is here, and I need a few minutes with her."

"I'm sorry, Mr. Green, but the Lt. Governor asked not to be disturbed today since she has back-to-back meetings all day. I can make an appointment with her tomorrow afternoon if you'd like."

"No, I'll try again tomorrow."

"Would you like to leave her a message?"

"Yes, tell her I was here and ask her to call me. She has my number.

Frank leaves disappointed that he couldn't see Morgan. He returns to his hotel and calls her, but his call goes straight to voicemail.

He is so upset that he goes to a local bar, gets drunk, and tries to start fights with customers. Before the tavern closes, the bartender notices Green's hotel key with his money on the bar top and calls a cab to take him back to his hotel before he gets into a fight with a customer.

The crooked cab driver takes Green to an alley and pulls him out of the vehicle. The cabby beats him up before taking all his money, valuables, and identification, then drives away, leaving Green all bloody in the alley.

The following morning, Green wakes with a pounding hangover and tries to stand. After realizing his legs aren't working, he crawls to the street. A pedestrian sees him on the ground and calls the police and an ambulance. The paramedics took him to the nearest hospital.

"What is your name?" the police asked him in the emergency room.

"My name is Frank Green, and I'm staying at the local hotel, but I can't remember which one. Where is my room key?"

"Do you remember what happened to you last night?"

"I remember going to a bar for a drink, but everything else is fuzzy. I must have blacked out."

"The doctor wants you to stay here to check you out for a couple of hours. It seems you were mugged and left in the alley. We'll try to find your hotel and the bar you were in," the policeman said. "Do you want us to call anyone for you?"

"Yes, could you call the Lt. Governor and tell her I'm here?"

"Why do you want to talk to the Lt. Governor?"

"She is my friend, and she can get me back to my hotel," Green said.

The police look at each other confused but call Mrs. Eastman's office and explain the situation to the secretary.

"I will give the information to Mrs. Eastman when she returns from lunch," the secretary said.

Eastman returned to her office and told her security guards to go to the hospital and tell Mr. Green that he must go home immediately and not contact her again.

After hearing from the security guards, Green is confused. He thought Morgan loved him and would be happy to see him. The police gave him the name of his hotel earlier in the day. The doctors treated his injuries and released him after all his tests came back normal.

Before leaving the hospital, Green calls his credit card companies and reports them stolen. One company issues him a new credit card number until he gets a new card that will be sent to him in the mail.

Green purchases a new phone, returns to his hotel, and calls the Lt. Governor.

"Why are you calling me? Didn't you get the message from my security guards?"

"I missed you and wanted to spend Valentine's Day with you," Frank said.

"Are you out of your mind? Why did you come to Tallahassee? How often have I told you we must be discreet? she said. "And you were here at my office. My husband is home from deployment and often visits me at my office. Now, go home and leave me alone. I don't want you to call me anymore. Do you understand?"

Green knows she didn't mean her words, but he still feels rejected. So, he goes home to sulk.

Chapter 23

Edward Moore saddled his thoroughbred Black Dominoes and routinely rode him down the horse trail for exercise before the trainer started the horses' training routine.

Moore enjoys riding his horse when he is startled by someone jumping out of the bushes and into his path.

"What are you doing here? You surprised me," Moore said to the person.

The individual grabbed the horse's bridle and shot Moore. The rider fell off the horse, and the shooter quickly picked up his brass and rode away with the horse.

It takes an hour before the trainer realizes Mr. Moore has not returned with the horse. The trainer rides his horse to the horse trail, discovers the body, and calls the police.

Wagner and Steele arrived at the scene.

"You discovered the body?" Steele asked the trainer.

"Yes, sir. Mr. Moore's routine is to take his thoroughbred for a walk to warm up the horse before training. When he didn't return, I looked for him. I called the police and an ambulance when I found him."

"Did you touch anything?" Steele asked.

"No, I didn't touch or move anything. I watch enough cop shows to know that."

"Did you get the horse?"

"When I got here, the horse was gone. The stallion is a three-year-old Arabian with a chestnut coat named Black Dominoes. We must find the horse because he qualified for the Kentucky Derby. The horse has a good chance of winning the Triple Crown because it has a lot of stamina, is talented, and has a good trainer. Mr. Moore was confident that this horse would win the Triple Crown this year," the trainer said.

Parker arrives as the trainer turns to leave.

"Excuse me. My name is Ashley Parker from the *Ocala Star Banner*. Are you the one that found the body?"

The trainer told her the same information that he had given to Steele.

"How do you get to the scene so fast?" Steele asks after the trainer leaves.

"Did you forget I have a police scanner at my desk?"

"Right. You did tell me last year that you had one."

"This man looks familiar. Is he one of the ranchers?"

"He is Edward Moore from the Black House of Dominoes Ranch," Steele said.

"He has a gunshot wound to his upper body. Someone didn't rob him because he still has his ring and watch. The wallet in his back pocket shows that this is Moore," Wagner said.

"How long ago do you think someone killed him?"

"With his liver temp and lack of rigor, I would say he died about one to two hours ago."

"This is starting to look like a pattern. The first two victims were scared off their horses, and the next two, somebody shot them," Parker said.

"Let's not jump to conclusions before the coroner does the autopsy."

"But, Steele, someone obviously shot him in the chest. You can see the hole in his chest and all the blood," Parker said.

The coroner's assistant arrived, and Wagner helped put Mr. Moore in the body bag and take him to the morgue for an autopsy.

Wagner and Steele search the area for clues, with Parker behind them.

"There isn't anything here. The perp didn't leave anything. And the horse's hoof tracks blur any human footprints."

"Well, I have enough information for a good story. I'll call you after the coroner finishes the autopsy to get the details," Parker said to Steele as she left.

Chapter 24

Nancy texts Steele about visiting for a few days to spend Valentine's Day together. She tells him that she has already made reservations at the same hotel where she stayed before and will be there on February 13 in the afternoon if he is available.

Steele responds that he will take a half-day off and looks forward to her visit.

He arrives in time to take her to dinner. They embraced and kissed in the lobby.

"It's only been a few weeks since we were together, but it seems like it has been months. I missed you so much," Nancy said.

"I agree with you, and we will have to find different ways to spend more time together."

They go to the Don Pepe Mexican restaurant in Dunnellon. While waiting on the restaurant's porch for a table, Erin Kelly and Ashley Parker arrive.

"Hi, Nancy. It's good to see you again. This is Erin Kelly, my roommate."

"Nice to meet you. Grant, why don't you tell the hostess that we want a table for four," Nancy said.

"Already on it," he says with a smile as he gets up to make the change.

"Erin just started a new job at the historic Ocala Manor Hotel downtown," Parker said. "She used to work at the Cosmopolitan

Hotel in the Villages until it was closed by the cops."

"I remember the police discovered the money laundering going on there and closed the hotel."

Steele returns to the porch and tells the ladies their table is ready. They enter the small restaurant with tables, chairs, and booths all with a Mexican décor. Big straw sombreros decorate the restaurant's walls, and red pepper and chili-printed curtains cover some windows. After giving the waiter their orders, they continue talking while munching on warm, crispy corn tortilla chips with spicy salsa and drinking Mexican beer.

"So, how do you like the area and your new job?" Nancy asks Erin.

"It's excellent, but there appears to be something mysterious going on at the hotel. I just can't figure out what it is."

"What do you mean mysterious?" Steele asks.

"There are many doors marked for employees only, but the keys they gave me won't open some of the doors or the basement. It's weird."

"Did you ask about it?" Steele asks.

"I did, but the manager told me to leave those doors alone and mind my own business, which makes me question everything. There is a small restaurant and bar in the back of the hotel. Business people and guests fill it almost every night. But I've only been there for ten days. Maybe I'll figure out the mystery after more time."

"If you figure out what it's all about, let me know," Steele said.

"Oh no. If Erin finds out anything, she will tell me first so I can have another great story," Parker said.

"Okay but keep me informed on anything you discover."

"That won't be a problem. You will know right after I tell Ashley," Erin said.

As they finished dinner, Ashley noticed Nancy's ring.

"Oh, your ring is beautiful. When is the wedding date?"

"We haven't set a date yet. I still have to pay off the ring,"

Steele said jokingly.

"We really haven't discussed a date yet. We have many things to work out before we can set a date," Nancy said.

"Do you remember Chuck Vaughn? Ashley asks Steele.

"Sure, he was the physical therapist beaten in the alley in The Villages, and you became friendly with him while he was in the hospital. Why do you ask?"

"Kelly went back for more therapy on her knee, and Chuck took care of her and asked for my address and phone number. He sent me a dozen long-stemmed red roses for Valentine's Day. I got them today before we went out for dinner."

"Oh, that sounds interesting. Did Chuck say if he was coming here for a visit?" Nancy asks.

"The note with the flowers said he would see me soon."

"Oh, that sounds promising," Nancy said with a smile.

Chapter 25

The coroner texted Steele that the autopsy report on Edward Moore was ready.

Steele does Facetime with the coroner.

"Edward Moore was a normal sixty-five-year-old and weighed 200 pounds. His five-foot-ten-inch body was very muscular for a man his age and he suffered from chronic obstructive pulmonary disease. Everything else was normal; he could have lived for many more years. The cause of death was someone shot him in his chest at close range. It looks like someone used a 9mm handgun. It was probably a Glock. The perp shot upward from the ground while Mr. Moore sat on his horse."

"Thanks, Doc. Did you find the bullet?"

"No, the bullet went through and through. You'll have to look for it in the area where Mr. Moore was shot."

Steele thanks the doctor and goes to Wagner's office.

"Just what I need is to look in bushes and trees for a bullet," Steele mumbled and reminded himself to stop his mumbling.

"Hey, Wagner, do you want to ride to the Moore ranch with me and look for a bullet later?"

"Okay, I've finished my work for the day, and I enjoy watching the horses."

They drive on C.R. 328 until they reach the curving driveway with tall pines leading to the ranch.

The maid opened the wooden door with the elegant black feather wreath signifying a house of mourning.

"How may I help you Detective?" the maid asks, wiping away tears.

"We would like to see Mrs. Moore," Steele said.

'I'm sorry, but Miss Laura is lying down and not seeing visitors today."

"How long have you been working for Mr. and Mrs. Moore?" Steele asked as they entered the house.

"I have been with Miss Laura since her parents drowned in a boating accident when she was fifteen. Her grandparents took her in and hired me to be her nanny. I've been with her for five years now."

As Steele and the maid talk, Wagner notices Laura Moore gracefully walking down the grand staircase wearing a black velvet dressing gown with a white fur collar and black slippers. She is holding a lacey monogrammed handkerchief in her hand.

"Why are you in my house?" Laura Moore demands.

"I am Detective Grant Steele, and this is CSI Jack Wanger from the sheriff's office. We hope you can talk to us about your husband."

"What do you want to know about my husband?" Mrs. Moore said as she slowly walked to the couch. "Please sit and ask your questions."

"Did your husband have any enemies?'

"No, everybody loved him. My husband was a good man dedicated to raising thoroughbred horses to win big races. Some people may have envied him because of his ability to find good horses and train jockeys to ride them," she said. "But no one had any reason to kill him."

"Did your husband have any problems with the other ranchers?"

"No, he was trying to get a jockey that worked for the Green Oaks Ranch, but I don't know if he was able to get him," she said.

"Do you remember the jockey's name?"

"No, he never told me his name. But he is supposed to be the best jockey here, and Ed needed him to ride our thoroughbred."

"Did your husband gamble or owe money to anyone?"

"Of course not. Edward was an honest and wealthy man. He didn't owe money to anyone, and I resent you talking like that about my husband. Leave my house now."

"Miss Laura, please calm yourself," the maid said. "Should I call the doctor?"

"No, just usher the gentlemen out of my house and help me back to bed."

Steele and Wagner leave as the maid helps Mrs. Moore.

"Are you ready to go and look for the bullet? I don't think we'll get anywhere with the wife or the maid," Steele said after they left.

"Let's get out there before it gets dark. We won't be able to find anything in the dark."

"Maybe we will get lucky tonight and find the missing bullet."

They checked the area where they found Moore. They look all over the ground and shrubs and finally find the bullet stuck, about six feet up in a tree trunk. Using his knife, Steele removes the shell, which is badly damaged.

"It doesn't look like this is going to be very helpful. The bullet is distorted so that a comparison will be impossible."

Chapter 26

The killer of Edward Moore decided to save the thoroughbred, Black Dominoes, instead of sending him to be slaughtered. The horse has been trained and destined to win the Kentucky Derby. He is a horse lover and can't live with himself if he sends the classic thoroughbred to be destroyed.

He looked online to find a horse buyer out of the country. He finds a rich Pakistani man in Dubai willing to pay a small fortune to own a trained horse with a lineage that someone can trace to the Darley Arabian sires, making this a valuable horse.

They communicate back and forth until all the arrangements are completed. He also ensures the tattoo on the horse's lip is changed just enough so somebody can't trace Black Dominoes back to Moore's ranch, but they can still trace the horse's lineage.

The killer hires a private international horse transport plane to take him and the horse to Dubai. They arrive after a thirteen-hour plane ride. A small Pakistani man wearing loose white linen trousers with a white polo shirt and suede sneakers waits on the tarmac with a woman wearing a pair of loose trousers with a matching tunic and a scarf on her head standing behind him. The man anxiously rubs his hands together as someone walks the horse off the plane's rear exit ramp.

"This horse is fifteen hands and has a finely chiseled bone structure, large dark eyes, and a high carried tail. This horse is more than I had hoped," the pleased buyer said. "My administrator will give you the bank account number to the offshore account where the money we agreed upon has been deposited in your name. Would you join me for lunch before you leave?"

"Thank you, but I'll have to refuse. I'm on a tight schedule."

"Possibly the next time. Please call again if you find another thoroughbred horse you are willing to sell. I will make it worth your while."

The killer completes his business, takes a different private plane back to the United States, and does everything he can to cover his tracks.

After he returns to his ranch, exhausted, he gets a text from the ranch committee informing him that a meeting will be held today in the WEC meeting room at 2 p.m., and he needs to be there.

Steele and Wagner also get an invite to the meeting to discuss the details of Moore's death and the robbery of Helen Lane.

Everyone shows up, and Frank Green opens the meeting on time. Ashley Parker quietly enters the room and sits in the back, taking notes.

Steele tells the ranchers that unknown subjects robbed Helen Lane's boarding stable of six boarded horses and all their tack on Christmas Eve. And that the horse, Black Diamond, is also missing. He's concerned about the black market selling of horse meat.

"Right now, we don't have any evidence connecting anyone to the murders or the theft of all the horses. We also don't know if the two crimes are even connected," Steele said. "Anyone with any ideas or information of who could have committed these crimes should contact me."

"Now, we have some serious business to discuss. Someone will have to talk to Mrs. Moore. We need to know if she will enter any of her other thoroughbred horses in the upcoming races or give up her rancher's silks since someone killed her husband. I don't think she has anyone else to take over for him or another horse ready to compete," Green said. "But Moore liked to keep secrets, so we don't know if he has a thoroughbred ready to qualify."

"I don't understand what silks mean," Steele said.

"'Silks' refer to the colors the jockeys wear during the races. They consist of a shirt worn over their required protective vests that must be tucked into their pants and a cap that covers the jockey's safety helmet. They represent the owner of the horse like a uniform represents a team. It also allows the race commentators to differentiate easily between racehorses," Green said. "Now, who would be willing to talk to Mrs. Moore?"

"I could talk to Laura Moore on Tuesday," Helen Lane said. "I'm sure everyone will be going to her husband's funeral on Saturday, so that will give her a few days to grieve before I go to visit her. I'm sure she would rather talk to a woman than a man under the circumstances."

"Good. Thank you, Helen, for volunteering. We appreciate it," Green said. "If there isn't any other business, we will adjourn the meeting. If you find any evidence or knowledge about Detective Steele's crimes, please call him. Thank you for coming."

Steele and Wagner stop and talk to Parker as everyone else leaves.

"What's going on?" Steele asks.

"The ranchers always get excited when competing in races nationwide and worldwide. Points are given to the top four finishers in each race. The horse can only be three years old to qualify. That is why the Kentucky Derby is a once-in-a-lifetime event for horses and their owners. They train and compete all year to get points to qualify for the Derby, which is always held the first weekend in May," Parker said. "Most treat their horses like family and want to know if there is a problem so they can stop it before it happens."

"Thanks for the explanation. Wagner and I have to search again for clues. We just can't find them," Steele said.

"As the Derby race gets closer, there will be even more excitement for the owners, trainers, grooms, and jockeys," Parker said. "Good luck. I have a story to write if I want the information from this meeting to appear in tomorrow's paper. See you later."

Chapter 27

Chuck Vaughn and Ashley Parker have been communicating via texts for several weeks. The friendship they built while Vaughn was in the hospital recovering from his beating had developed into more than an acquaintance. Vaughn sent Parker a dozen long-stemmed red roses for Valentine's Day, and he feels it is time for them to get together to talk in person.

"I would like to visit with you for a few days. Can you recommend a hotel that would be close to you?" Vaughn texts.

"You can go to the Comfort Inn and Suites Hotel in Dunnellon. Nancy Jennings stays there when she visits Grant," Parker texted back.

"Good. I'm taking a few days off starting on March 1. Will you be available to spend some time with me?"

"Of course. I'll also take a couple of days off. We'll have a good time. I can take you to the Rainbow Springs State Park and show you around the town," Parker said.

Parker is five-foot-three inches tall and meets six-foot Vaughn in the hotel lobby, and they embrace.

"I didn't realize you were so tall. I guess you were always sitting in therapy or lying in a hospital bed when I was with you," Parker said.

"I have wanted to hug you some time ago, and I'm glad it's finally happening," Vaughn said.

"I agree with you, Chuck. We should have done this long ago."

Walking hand in hand, Parker took him to enjoy some jumping events at the World Equestrian Center. She also escorted him to the state park, and they spent the day walking and enjoying the beautiful scenery. She then drove him to the historic Ocala district, where they visited Erin at the Ocala Manor Hotel.

"It is nice to see you again, Erin. Maybe the three of us could go out to dinner tonight. I appreciated you caring for my cat while I was in the hospital," Vaughn said.

"That would be great. I'll leave at 6 p.m. and can meet you at the restaurant. Where do you want to go for dinner?" Erin asks.

They agreed to meet at the Olive Garden in Ocala.

The three enjoy a delicious Italian dinner with salad, soup, and garlic bread sticks. They continued discussing the past and future plans over a glass of white Zinfandel.

"We've been talking about a five-day cruise to the Bahamas leaving from Port Canaveral. We would leave about the middle of March and enjoy some warm weather," Parker said.

"Oh, this is getting serious. Is that why you didn't come home the last few nights?"

"Yes, if you have to be so nosey," Ashley said with a smile.

"That would be fantastic. You'll get to know each other while on a cruise. I'm sure I can hold down the fort while you're gone," Erin said happily.

Vaughn took Parker home, checked out of his hotel, traveled to his home in the Villages, and planned to return to Dunnellon for the cruise. Chuck makes arrangements for his neighbor to keep his cat while he is away.

The days slowly pass for Chuck and Ashley as they await their cruise departure date.

Chuck returns to town, picks up Ashley, and both leave Ocala for their cruise. They spend their time on the ship doing various activities in the afternoon, dancing in the evenings, and getting to know each other better. The days quickly pass, and the cruise ends on an important note for the couple. They return well-rested, tanned, and in love.

Significant changes are happening at the Ocala Manor Hotel, and Erin anxiously waits for Parker to return so she can tell her all about it. She also wants to hear all the news about their trip.

Chapter 28

Steele and Wagner head out to the horse trail from S.R. 40, looking for clues. Walking around, Steele decided they should try a different route. They left C.R. 328 and drove down to the abandoned road. They drive around the bend and find a lot of debris on the side of the road.

"This is interesting. Get out the evidence bags and collect everything," Steele said.

"We have candy papers, sandwich wrappers, empty soda cans, empty water bottles, and a lot of garbage. Why would anyone leave all this smelly trash?" Wagner asks. "Do you have binoculars in your car?"

"Sure. What do you want to see?"

"Let's see what is on the other side of these tall pine trees and bushes."

"Good point. You aren't going to believe what I can see," Steele said, looking through the binoculars. "It is the Double H Boarding Ranch. Someone was watching the stables, and from the amount of litter, they were here for several days, if not weeks."

"The tall grass on the shoulder is packed down and brown, so they were here for a long time," Wagner said. "It also looks like they were using the shoulder as a bathroom. The grass is all yellow in that one area.

Both men don vinyl gloves and put the litter in evidence bags to take back to the lab.

"Let's get this trash picked up and hopefully get some answers."

Returning to his office, Wagner is anxious to start categorizing each item and hopes to get some DNA or fingerprints off the trash.

Working into the night, Wagner cataloged several sets of fingerprints. He planned to work on the DNA samples the following day.

Steele reported to work on Wednesday and checked in with Wagner.

"Did you find anything we can use to determine who was doing the stakeout?"

"All my fingerprints do not match anything in the system. The prints are small, so I would guess they belong to children. The perps weren't ever fingerprinted for any reason. So, they aren't criminals, in the military, or had fingerprints taken in elementary school."

"Why would kids have their fingerprints taken in elementary school?" Steele asks.

"There was a program called Ident-A-Kid. The police took every child's prints to use if anyone abducted the child. With the prints, they also took a picture of the child and put their eye, hair color, and other info on the special card. Most parents had the cards laminated if someone ever needed them."

"I wonder why I never heard of this program?"

"Someone started the program in 1986 in St. Petersburg, Florida. If the program still exists, I'm sure everything is digital now."

"Since you're speaking about kids, this debris looks like junk food kids would eat," Steele said.

"You might be onto something. Maybe we should contact the Social Worker and find out why the Cobb kids aren't in school or if they somehow finished their education already."

"Good idea. Are you ready to go for a ride to find some answers?"

Steele plugs in his GPS to find the shortest route to the Marion County Department of Children and Families. Finding Beverly Thorne, the social services lady caring for the Cobb children, took a while.

"I'm Detective Steele, and this is CSI Wagner," Steele said, showing her his I.D. and badge.

"How can I help you, Detective?"

"We're interested in four of your clients, the Cobb children. We're curious why the younger Cobb children aren't in school?"

"They aren't in school because I can't make them go to school. Besides, the schools are on Spring break right now. Every time I find a way for them to attend school, they just don't go. I have thirty cases that I'm responsible for, which include eighty children. I do my best, but I can't be everywhere at once."

"I didn't realize you were in charge of so many people," Steele said.

"The Cobb children are doing well taking care of each other, and now that their mother is back, things should be better."

"I'm sorry to inform you, but I arrested Mrs. Cobb yesterday, and she will probably go to jail for a while."

"Well, it's a good thing I didn't close their file. Otherwise, I would have to do a lot of paperwork to open a new file on them. I'll update my report on the Cobb family," she said. "Thanks for informing me. I'll return them to my visitation list and continue to see them monthly."

"That would be good. Please keep me informed on the children's activities," Steele said, giving her his card. "I want to be notified of any changes for the children."

"Yes, sir. I can keep you up to date with the children."

Chapter 29

Paula Drake and Helen Lane meet at noon on March 15 for their usual monthly lunch get-together. The waiter greets them when they enter the posh golf course restaurant.

"Good afternoon, ladies. I have reserved your favorite table overlooking the golf course. I also took the liberty of pouring a glass of Chardonnay for each of you," José, the waiter, said.

"José, you are the best. What is your special today?" Paula asks, as they sit at the table.

"We have prime rib with twice-baked potatoes and green beans," he said.

"Oh, that sounds delicious. We will both have that and make them medium rare if that is okay with you, Helen."

"That's fine with me."

"Excellent choice," the waiter said.

The ladies relax with their wine and start talking about their problems.

"My husband is so upset that somebody killed Willie Flynn. Everyone was trying to hire Willie because he was the best jockey around here," Paula said. "Willie didn't take my husband's offer to work and ride for him either."

"Is he trying to find another jockey?" Helen asks.

"He has been working on finding another jockey for months and hasn't been successful yet. He is so upset and difficult to be around. It's like he is preoccupied all the time. Okay, that is enough about me. Tell me how your daughter is doing with her kidney problems."

"After a while, the doctor decided to cut through her back, open the kidney, remove the stones, and then put in a tube for three weeks to keep the incision open. She was in agony for those three weeks. She couldn't move because the stent was so painful. Finally, the doctor took the stent out, and the pain subsided. After all that, Cat passed a kidney stone one week later. So far, nothing else has worked," Helen said. "The doctor said he could save the kidney with this procedure because the kidney wasn't badly damaged."

"Well, that is awful. By the way, you never told me why you call your daughter Cat?"

"When she was born, her eyes were gold like a cat's. I wanted to name her Cat, but Howard wouldn't go along with it. So, I named her Catherine after her great-great-grandmother and called her Cat. Even now, her eyes change to green or blue depending on what color she wears."

"I've always wondered about her name."

She is doing better. She will just have to be like this for the rest of her life," Helen said.

"At least she doesn't have to worry about losing her kidney. That is good news," Paula said.

"Yes, we are so grateful."

Have you heard how Laura is doing since someone killed her husband?" Paula asks.

"No, I haven't seen her since Frank Green requested someone to see her, and I volunteered to talk to her about whether she was keeping her family silks. She was distraught then, but I hadn't seen her since. Maybe we should be neighborly and visit her," Helen said.

"She is so young, and we don't have anything in common, but let me think about it before I commit to visiting her."

"Now, Paula, you are a good person, and it wouldn't kill you to visit a grieving widow."

"Well, you never know.

Chapter 30

The Cobb children are sitting in their living room and discussing how they must make some money to get their mother out of jail.

"Selling all that horse tack didn't get much money," Doug said.

"That's because most of the people buying the tack figured we stole it since we look like a bunch of dirty little kids," Sally said.

"Why don't you call the boss back and tell him we need more money, or we're going to the cops," Steve said.

"That sounds like a great idea. Then he'll have to give us some money," Doug said. "If we go to the cops, won't we get in trouble for robbing the barn?"

"No, the boss will pay 'cause he got all the horses and doesn't want trouble with the cops," Sally said.

The kids all talk about the pros and cons of the idea until they all agree that Tommy should call the boss and ask for more money.

Tommy calls the boss and explains his demands to get more money for his work, or he goes to the cops.

The boss listens, tells Tommy to go where they left the stolen horses with his two men, and assures them they will get all the money they deserve. He tells them to be there in half an hour, and his men will be waiting for them.

"Great. He is going to give us money. I think we should all go together and collect our reward," Tommy said. "You stay here, Sally."

"Why do you guys always get to do the fun things, and I have to stay here?"

"There isn't enough room in the cab for all of us. That's why."

The three boys jump into the truck while Sally sulks in the doorway.

As Tommy's truck leaves the Romeo area, he accelerates onto Highway 41 for about a mile before an eighteen-wheeler speeds toward them and collides with the front of the boy's vehicle. The impact pushed the truck off the road into a tree in the gully. The tree stopped the mangled front of the pickup. The eighteen-wheeler leaves the scene. An eyewitness stopped, called 9-1-1 and reported the accident.

Steele and Wagner arrived with blue lights flashing and sirens blaring. They put on the vinyl gloves as they leave the patrol car. After seeing the demolished truck, Steele radios for and a tow truck. He then puts out orange cones to keep traffic from the crash area and talks to the eyewitness.

"Are you alright? May I have your license and insurance papers?"

"I'm fine. Here is my driver's license."

"Now, can you tell me what you saw?"

"I was southbound on Highway 41 with the pickup about five or six car lengths ahead of me when I saw this eighteen-wheeler barreling northbound. He moved into the southbound lane, hit the pickup, and returned to the northbound lane. I slammed on my brakes, moved to the shoulder, and managed to stay out of its way. It happened so fast. I thought he would hit me too," the witness said. "It looked like he was aiming to hit the truck."

"Do you remember anything about the eighteen-wheeler?"

"The only thing I remember is that the truck didn't have a trailer, just the cab of the eighteen-wheeler. I was so scared. I thought the cab would hit me too," she said, trembling.

"Thanks for your time and for reporting the crash. You appear to be in shock. Are you okay to drive?"

"I already called my husband, he's on the way to pick me up and have someone else drive my car home. I'll be fine."

All three boys were not wearing seat belts and were thrown from the truck. Wagner tries to help the boys until the paramedics arrive. He looked up at Steele and slowly moved his head from side to side. Steele acknowledges that at least one boy is dead, and he radios that the medical assistant, and the Florida Highway Patrol are also needed.

He also tells the dispatcher to take out a BOLO for the cab of an eighteen-wheeler that may or may not have front end damage.

The TV crews arrive and set up across from the scene to film the wreck. The paramedics went to the wrecked truck and confirmed that all three boys were thrown from the vehicle and had died from their injuries.

At the trailer, Sally anxiously paces the floor for an hour, waiting for her brothers to return with the money.

"What is possibly taking them so long to pick up some money," she says to herself. Sally is impatiently waiting until she hears a vehicle approaching the house. She runs outside to see a black Dodge Ram truck that she didn't recognize.

Sally stands in her doorway, watching the truck approach their front door. The truck pulls next to the door, and the passenger jumps out and grabs Sally. And at five foot tall and weighing ninety pounds, he picks her up like a sack of potatoes. He throws her on the floor in the back of the vehicle, with her screaming and kicking the whole time.

"Put me down. What do you want?" Sally screams before the man holds her down until he puts duct tape on her mouth, tapes her wrists and ankles together, and covers her head with a hood.

She is lying on the back seat floor, crying, and trembling. The vehicle drives for a while before stopping. The man picked her up like a rag doll, took her inside a trailer, removed the hood, and dumped her on a dirty bed with a worn and torn mattress.

"All your brothers are dead, so be a good girl and stay put. If you give me any trouble, I'll kill you too, and you'll end up dead like your brothers. Do you understand?" the man asks as he heads to the door of the trailer.

Sally nods her head.

The closest neighbor to the Cobb's trailer notifies the police that someone took Sally out of her trailer screaming.

Steele had started a preliminary investigation into the accident when dispatch told Steele to check out an abduction in the area. He left Wagner to secure the scene until the Florida Highway Patrol arrived. He can get everything he needs for his incident report tomorrow from FHP. He drove to the latest call just down the road.

The neighbor tells Steele after he arrived, that she saw a black Dodge Ram pickup slowly driving past her house toward her neighbors, so she stepped onto her front porch, and then she heard Sally screaming.

"The Cobb children are usually very quiet, and I look out for them since they're alone. So, when I heard Sally scream bloody murder, I knew she was in trouble. That is when I saw two big white men in the truck," the neighbor said.

"Did you recognize them, or have you seen them before?" Steele asks.

"Never saw them before, but the passenger that grabbed Sally was a tall white man with long, shoulder-length black hair. He wore a dirty T-shirt, blue jeans, and bright blue cowboy boots."

"Did you happen to get a license number or anything unusual about the truck?" Steele asks.

"No, I didn't, but they had an NRA sticker on the back window, and the left brake light didn't work, but I don't remember anything else," she said.

"We appreciate any help we can get. Are there any other neighbors close by?"

"There are a few old trailers around here. I've been here for about a year. There are some other homes down the road, but I don't know if anyone lives in them."

"Thanks for your information. Would you go with me to check out Cobb's trailer?"

"Sure. I'm worried about the children."

Steele and the neighbor see the open front door and look inside the trailer, but nothing seems out of place.

"Thank you for your time. We'll check it out, but if Sally returns, call me," Steele said while he gave her his card and closed the front door before he left to pick up Wagner.

Chapter 31

Chuck and Ashley arrive at her apartment on Tuesday and relax with a glass of white Zinfandel while waiting for Erin to come home from work.

"Tell me all about your cruise, and then I have a lot of things to discuss with you," Erin said as she rushed into the apartment.

"Get a glass of wine, and I'll set up the pictures we took while in Bermuda," Ashley said. "Then I'll give you the details of our trip with each picture."

The couple shows picture after picture and gives explanations for each photo while Erin fidgets with her glass of wine.

"Okay, now tell me all your news before you explode," Ashley said.

First, Erin tells them about the three boys who died in an accident.

"According to the T.V. news, they were brothers but didn't appear to have any family. The reporters said they weren't orphans. It was confusing. All the T.V. stations covered the crash. It was big news. An eighteen-wheeler crossed the center line and struck a small truck. It was awful. All three teenage boys were thrown from their vehicle and died at the scene. They weren't wearing their seatbelts," Erin said. "You missed a good story."

"I'll call Steele in the morning and get the information and can still write a follow-up story. I'll also try to find out about the boy's parents.

"Okay, now, let me tell you about my work."

"Did something new happen?" Ashley asks.

"I checked with the Historical Society and found the hotel's history. The Howell family built the hotel in the early 1920s, and the owners had a speakeasy in the basement until prohibition ended. It was all very glamorous at the time."

"Wow, that is interesting. What else happened while we were gone?"

"Well, the manager just finished training all the housekeepers, and they were doing a good job. Then, right after you left for your cruise, nineteen girls were gone, but Maria was still there. She is an older woman who came with the first group and is now teaching twenty new girls how to clean and make beds," Erin said, taking a sip of wine. "All the new women were very young. I would think they are in their early teens or even younger. They were unkempt with long, dirty black hair. All of them were wearing flowered skirts, blouses, and flip-flops.

The afternoon manager spends her time helping teach the basics of cleaning to the new women and tells them what to do. None of them seem to know anything about housekeeping. And no one speaks English. I think they speak Spanish, but I'm not sure," Erin said. "I wish I paid more attention in the Spanish class in high school, and then at least I would know what they were saying."

"This is so exciting. Do you have any idea of what is going on? Have you been able to open the locked doors?" Chuck asks.

It is puzzling. My keys still don't fit all of the doors. Because of its history, I want to get into the basement, and I hear strange noises from there."

"What kind of strange noises?" Ashley asks.

"It's different kinds of noises. Sometimes, it sounds like moans, or it could be someone murmuring. Just weird noises that I can't make out, and it's only noticeable in the evenings."

"Oh, that is interesting. When did this all happen about getting the new girls?" Ashley asks.

"I always work the day shift, but the afternoon manager told me to go home early on Friday and take the weekend off, which was unusual."

"Why would that be unusual?" asks Ashley.

Friday is normally a busy day for us, and I haven't had the weekend off since I started working. We have a lot of reservations for Friday afternoon and the weekend. We must have all the paperwork ready because new guests arrive at about 3 p.m. on Friday. Besides, the manager was busy teaching the new girls about cleaning and wouldn't have time to do everything. That's why I said it was unusual for her to tell me to go home early."

"That does sound strange. Were you able to meet any of the new women?" Chuck asks.

"No, I don't talk to any of the housekeeping staff. Only the afternoon manager does that. I walked into the break room and saw them long enough to know they were all new before the manager told me to leave."

"That does sound strange. How were the new girls doing when you went back to work on Monday?' Chuck asks.

"It was weird. On Monday, all the girls were all cleaned up. They were all clean with short haircuts and wearing the hotel's uniform. They all looked different and even younger than when I first saw them, if possible. It was unbelievable that they changed so drastically in a few days. Maria was still showing the new women how to clean."

"There is something strange going on at the hotel. We just have to figure it out. Just be careful while you're working," Ashley said. "Maybe you should talk to Steele about this to see what he has to say."

"You know, that isn't a bad idea. I should call him tomorrow. Maybe he has an idea of what is going on there."

Chapter 32

Lt. Governor Morgan Eastman calls Frank to see if he wants to visit her home this evening.

"I'm so sorry about what happened in Tallahassee. Can you possibly forgive me?" she asks. "I'm in Ocala for a few days and want to spend quality time with you."

Frank is still upset, but anxious to spend time with Morgan again.

"You told me not to contact you again, which hurt my feelings," he said. "I'm supposed to just say that everything is okay now, and I forgive you?"

"Frank, I need to spend some time with you. My husband is on deployment again, so we won't be disturbed. Won't you reconsider and just come over?" she said.

After a few minutes, Frank finally surrenders to Morgan's pleading and tells her he'll be right over.

"Oh, that's wonderful. It has been a long time, so why don't you plan on spending the night? Although you will have to leave before my security car picks me up in the morning and my cleaning lady arrives," she said.

"I'll leave in a few minutes and pick up some champagne on the way."

"I'm waiting for you, dear."

Frank quickly packs his toiletries and heads to Morgan's house.

He parks his car a few houses down the street from her home and walks to the house. She greets him at the door, and they kiss before entering the house. He pops the cork and pours champagne into the glasses that Morgan had ready for them. They talk and enjoy their champagne. Then Frank takes her hand and heads to the bedroom. They slowly take off each other's clothes. Frank passionately kisses Morgan, and they fall onto the bed.

They make passionate love throughout the night and are exhausted in the morning. They shower together, and Frank leaves before Morgan's cleaning lady arrives.

During their evening of lovemaking, Morgan explains that she loves Frank, but if her husband found out about the affair, he would divorce her. The bad publicity would ruin her career. Besides, her husband would take everything, leaving her with nothing.

When they started their arrangement, they agreed that Morgan would not leave her husband for him. But Frank changes his mind and wants to confess to Morgan that he wants to marry her. He will wait until they meet again before he tells her about his change of heart and hopes she feels the same.

"That is why I have to be so careful. I hope you understand. Also, can we meet again in a few days?" Morgan asks as Frank leaves.

"Of course, it will be my pleasure to entertain you at my house. I will get someone to cater a meal for us and have them leave."

"That would be perfect. Now you have to leave. It is getting late, and my cleaning lady will be here shortly."

Frank kisses Morgan and quickly goes to his car, only to find a flat tire. He knows he can't call a towing service because he is parked down the street from her house. Frank doesn't have a choice but to change the tire himself. He manages to get the jack and spare out of the trunk before the security team drives by to pick up Morgan

"Do you need help changing the tire?" the security driver asks.

"No, thanks. I have everything under control," Frank said,

keeping his head down and not looking at the driver.

The men drive to Morgan's house, pick her up, and drive past Frank again on the way to the Lt. Governor's office.

He doesn't look up as the vehicle passes. He doesn't want the driver to recognize him. He is busy changing the tire. Frank then takes the flat to his favorite garage to get it fixed.

"It is a relatively new tire, but we live in Florida, and tires don't last as long in this heat," Frank said.

"There isn't anything wrong with this tire. I couldn't find any nails or objects that would flatten a tire," the mechanic said after inspecting the tire. "It appears someone let all the air out of the tire."

"I wonder who would do that," he said as the mechanic filled the tire with air to show no leaks as Frank's phone rang.

"Hello, darling. I saw you change your tire. Is everything okay?" Morgan asks.

"Do you have any juvenile delinquents in your neighborhood?"

"No, why do you ask?"

"My mechanic just told me that someone let the air out of the tire. Do you know anyone who would do that?"

"This is an old retirement neighborhood. We don't even have kids living around here.

"Why would anyone take the time to let the air out? Also, there were other cars parked on the street. Why was my car picked to vandalize?"

"I don't know, but I wanted to tell you the Governor wants me to hold another town meeting about the proposed road on Tuesday while I'm down here. Can you set up a meeting room and put out a notice to tell everyone about the meeting?"

"I will take care of it as soon as I get home. Do I have to worry about losing my property?"

"Of course not, darling. I love you and will take care of you."

Tuesday evening, anxious ranchers fill the meeting room. The Lt. Governor makes her grand entrance with the security guards.

The audience is all talking at once until the Lt. Governor approaches the podium. Everyone is talking about going to the Derby next week

Before she can speak, David Drake stands and asks her if there have been any changes since the last meeting.

"I'm sorry, but everything is the same as the last meeting. The Governor and I haven't made our decision about the proposed road yet," she said. "We are still getting input from the public."

"Well then, my wife and I are leaving. If you haven't stopped plans to build the road, we don't want to hear anything you have to say." Drake said as they quickly walked out of the meeting.

Other ranchers follow out after Drake leaves. Ashley Parker is the only one left in the room. She gets a quote from the Lt. Governor and leaves to write her story.

Frank Green approaches the Lt. Governor, and she tells her guards that they may go now as Green is taking her home.

Green discreetly brings his car to the rear of the building and picks up Mrs. Eastman. They drive to his home to enjoy the previously prepared meal. They quickly end up in bed and enjoy their stolen passion.

"We need to talk," Frank said.

"Well, that doesn't sound good," Morgan said, leaning on her elbow among the many pillows.

"I want to tell you that I love you and want you to leave your husband and marry me," Frank said as he lightly caressed her back.

"You know I can't do that. I told you that when we first began this affair. I won't leave Ted for any reason. Besides, you don't have any money, so you wouldn't be able to afford me," Morgan said as she got out of bed and began dressing.

"You always told me that you love me. You can't leave now. We have to talk," Frank said, holding his head.

"I'm sorry, Frank, there is nothing to talk about. You knew

when we started that we could never be together. Our wonderful affair and time together is over," Morgan said as she finished dressing.

"Please, Morgan, I love you. Don't leave me," he said, pacing the floor.

Devastated, Frank falls on the bed, holding his head, and sobs but refuses to cry as Morgan takes his car keys off the dresser and leaves him.

Chapter 33

Steele asks Wagner if he wants to go for a ride and talk to the ranchers. He eagerly agrees. They stop at Green's place, but Frank can barely open the door. He is upset and is nursing a hangover from drinking too much after Morgan left him last night.

"I have a few questions for you," Steele said. "But you don't look well. Are you okay?"

"I think I'm sick. Can you come back tomorrow?"

"Sure. Do you need help getting to a doctor?"

"No, I just need some sleep, and I'll be okay."

"We will see you tomorrow. Now, get yourself to bed."

As they leave, Steele gets a call from dispatch telling him Laura Moore wants to talk to him.

When they arrive, the maid tells them they can find Miss Laura in the barn. When Steele and Wagner enter the barn, they are surprised to see Laura dressed in jeans, a long-sleeved western blouse, a Stetson hat, and cowboy boots. She is vigorously brushing one of the horses.

"Thank you for coming so quickly. I asked you here to tell you I'm offering a $10,000 reward for any information leading to the arrest and conviction of the person that killed my husband."

Hearing the information, Steele walked behind the horse to get to the other side so he could face Laura. The animal steps back and slams Steele against the stall wall. Laura pulls the horse away as Steele moans and falls. After Wagner calls the ambulance, he explains to Steele that you never walk behind a horse without touching the horse's rump to let him know you are behind him.

The paramedics put Steele on a gurney and put him in the ambulance against his wishes.

"I don't need to go to the hospital," Steele said, gasping for air. "I don't like hospitals, and I'm okay."

"Just go with them and get checked out. You could be seriously injured. I will follow you to the hospital."

After seeing the results of the X-rays, the doctor informs Steele that he is lucky.

"You don't have any broken ribs, but you must rest for a while. You have bruised your chest and lungs. It will take several days before your breathing becomes normal again. It is important that you rest and not do any work or heavy lifting," the doctor said.

"Don't worry, doctor, I'll make sure that he'll rest," Wagner said.

He takes Steele home and calls Nancy to tell her the news. She said she would be there that evening to take care of him.

"Tell her that won't be necessary. I can take care of myself," Steele said as he struggled to sit up and breathe.

"It would be nice to have Nancy here," he mumbled, reminding himself to stop this bad habit.

Steele was resting on the couch when Nancy arrived with a bottle of Jack Daniels for medicinal purposes.

"Darling, are you okay? I'll stay until you are better," she said as she kissed him.

"I'm glad you are here, but you don't have to fuss over me. I'll be okay. Thanks for the Jack Daniels."

"You weren't kidding when you said your studio apartment was small, but I'll manage. How can you live in such a small place?"

"I told you it was the only place I could find to rent."

"Wagner told me what happened, and I can't believe you didn't know that you had to touch a horse's rump to let him know you were there."

"How was I supposed to know that? I've never been close to a horse before I moved here."

"Okay, let's get you settled. First, let's get you to bed. I will sleep on the couch while I'm here. Then I'll fix you some dinner. I hope you have some food in the house."

"I'm not home enough to cook. It's easier to eat out."

Nancy checks Steele's refrigerator and discovers an almost empty refrigerator with old, moldy take-out boxes and a few beers. Since there wasn't any food in the house, she ordered take-out. While waiting for the food to arrive, she cleans out the refrigerator.

Later after eating a warm meal, Nancy scolds Steele about being careful around horses.

"You need to learn about horses. They are large animals and can easily hurt you, as you have found out." After dinner, Nancy goes to the store to stock up on healthy food to fill his refrigerator and pantry.

Nancy takes care of Steele for several days. She keeps the work visits with Wagner to a minimum so he can rest and heal.

"I don't understand why Mrs. Moore is offering a reward. Doesn't she know how many crank phone calls we'll get now?" Steele tells Wagner.

"Well, I won't have to deal with the phone calls. That's on you and anyone you can get to help with the calls."

Steele tried to figure out why Mrs. Moore was so different from the last time he saw her and why she offered a reward. He wants to talk to Moore's maid and discover what is happening with Mrs. Moore. Steele decides that is the top priority after he has recuperated.

After another day, he is doing better and has decided to get back to work, so Nancy leaves with a promise to return soon for a visit.

Steele called Wagner to pick him up the following day so they could return to work.

Chapter 34

Chuck Vaughn calls Ashley to set up another visit. He wants to schedule a visit and plans to spend the week with her if she agrees. After weeks of thinking and planning, Chuck wants to discuss his future with her. Also, he would like to bring his cat if Ashley doesn't mind.

"Erin will love to see your cat again. She enjoyed taking care of him when you were in the hospital. You are both welcome any time."

Chuck makes the arrangements to meet at the hotel in the middle of May.

After anxiously waiting for Chuck, Ashley arrives at the hotel, and they hug and kiss.

"I have missed you so much," Chuck said. "It has been too long since we last met. I have so much to talk to you about."

They return to Ashley's place, and Chuck takes his gray cat out of his carrier.

"Let's get Lucky to set up in the other room so she will feel at home here."

They settle the cat in the next room and return to the front room.

"It's only been over a year since we met in the hospital, but I've seen how loving you can be when you took care of me. I love you and want you to be my wife," Chuck said as he opened a black velvet ring box with a diamond engagement ring.

"Oh, Chuck, it is beautiful. I would be honored to be your wife," Ashley said as he slipped the ring on her finger.

"First, I must tell you that I was married for three years, before she divorced me," Chuck said.

"Why did you get divorced? Was it because you couldn't get along?"

"At first, we got along just fine, but after a while, she decided that she liked women more than men. She said she couldn't stand for a man to touch her anymore. So, we got a divorce, and now she is happily living with another woman."

"I'm sorry that happened. I should also tell you that I was engaged for about a year until he decided to take a job opportunity in another state and didn't invite me to go along with him."

"I'm sorry. I'm sure that won't happen again because I'm staying here with you."

"That's good news."

"Now, let's talk about our future. I spoke to Drew Spencer about opening a therapy office in Dunnellon. He said that I could buy a Hands-On Physical Therapy office franchise. But he's not happy that I'll leave the shop and move here," Chuck said. "He is thinking of offering his franchise to other physical therapists. He would also let me use his invention of the No Pain Freeze lotion, which stops the pain of sore muscles. Hopefully, newly licensed therapists will take advantage of this opportunity. I said I would give him some names of therapists I knew in New York before I left and moved to Florida. Drew said he would give me a finder's fee for everyone that took his offer."

"That is a great idea and an easy way to make money. I can help you look for a location to set up shop here, close to Ocala's hospitals," Ashley said. "We shouldn't have a problem finding an office space near the hospitals."

"That is wonderful. After I get the franchise started, we can set a wedding day. So, we have to start finding a suitable location for me."

"You can also stay here until we can find an apartment together. It will be manageable, but we should check with Erin first. I don't want her to think I'm kicking her out."

"Let's take her out to dinner when she gets home from work, and we can talk about our living arrangements," Chuck said.

Erin arrives after work and is surprised to see Chuck sitting on the couch.

"Hi, Chuck. When did you arrive?"

"I just got here, and we were getting ready to go out to dinner. Would you like to join us?" Chuck asks.

All three go out to dinner and Ashley brings up the possibility of Chuck moving in with them.

"Would it be okay with you if Chuck lived here until we found a place of our own?" Ashley asks.

"That would be okay with me. Is that an engagement ring on your hand?" Erin asks.

Ashley explains that Chuck will open a therapy shop here, and they will marry after his shop opens and he gets established.

"Oh, that is wonderful. Am I going to be the maid of honor? When is the wedding?"

"I don't think we want a big wedding, but yes, you are my maid of honor. Chuck and I have not made any plans yet. You'll be the first to know when we set a wedding date, but it probably won't be until September or later. We have a lot of work to do."

After dinner they go back to the hotel. Chuck checks out and brings all his belongings to Ashley's apartment.

Erin is pleased to see Lucky walking around when they return.

Chapter 35

Since the doctor restricts Steele from driving for a few more days, it was arranged for Wagner to pick him up to visit Moore's ranch so they can talk with the maid.

"Something is going on with Mrs. Moore. First, her husband tells us that she is sickly and bedridden, then we see her brushing a horse just a few weeks after somebody murdered her husband," Steele said. "Nothing makes sense, and I'll bet the maid knows what's going on there."

"Why do you think she knows anything?"

"Because maids and butlers know everything that goes on in the house where they work."

They arrive at Moore's ranch and find the maid in the house.

"I'm sorry, but Miss Laura is in the barn with her horse."

"We came here to ask you questions about Miss Laura. We are getting two versions of Mrs. Moore's health?" Steele tells the maid. "Can you tell us what is going on here?"

"I shouldn't be talking about my mistress."

"We are only trying to find out who killed her husband, and I know you can help us. So, please tell us about her past."

After some hesitation, the maid finally tells Steele about her employer.

"Well, I already told you that her grandparents spoiled Miss Laura after her parents drowned in a boating accident when she was fifteen. The grandparents were elderly and unable to care for a teen, so they hired me as her nanny. Miss Laura quickly realized she could get anything she wanted because her grandparents felt great remorse. After all, her parents died after borrowing the grandparents' boat. Her parents didn't know how to swim and refused to wear life jackets. They drank heavily, and when the boat struck the shore, the impact threw the couple into the water, and they drowned. The grandparents gave Miss Laura anything she wanted. Then she met Edward Moore through the horse racing crowd, and they married soon after. Fortunately, her husband kept me on as Miss Laura's maid. At first, she was happy that he was rich and had a big ranch. She didn't mind that her husband was almost forty years her senior. She was twenty-one when she married Mr. Moore, but after about a year, Miss Laura told her husband that she wasn't feeling well and often stayed in bed. Several doctors examined her and said she was clinically depressed. Her persistent sadness caused her difficulty sleeping, poor appetite, and no energy, so she stayed in bed, and her husband accepted her behavior. He gave her the best doctors and medical care that money could buy," the maid said.

"All the doctor's diagnoses were the same?"

"Yes, Mr. Moore obtained the best doctors for her from all over the world. He often said that money was no object if the doctors could cure her. All the doctors agreed on her diagnosis. They gave her different kinds of medication and put her into therapy. She had been like this for about five years until her husband died last month. Now, she seems to be just fine. The doctors are puzzled about her recovery."

"Thank you for all this information. It has been very beneficial."

"Well, I never expected that kind of info. I wonder how many others are hiding secrets around here?" Steele said to Wagner as they returned to their car.

Chapter 36

The day after kidnapping Sally and taking her to the abandoned trailer, the two hefty men brought her some fast food and told her they killed her brothers by crashing into their truck. The man said he would also kill her if she didn't obey them. While restraining her, they used a long chain hooked high on the wall and secured her at the ankle with a leather cuff at the end of the heavy chain.

They tear the tape from her mouth, wrists, and ankles. They threaten that no one will hear her if she screams, but they will beat her to keep her quiet.

She nods her head in agreement. The men head out for a while and bring her a sack of hamburgers with a soda.

Sally is scared and hungry and cautiously takes the hamburgers from the men and hungrily eats and drinks the soda.

"The boss said we have to keep you healthy, so make sure you eat everything," one of the men said.

While Sally is eating, the men drink beer and joke around at the other end of the filthy trailer. After a few beers, the men return to Sally and tell her she did a good job by finishing all her food. They allow her to use the toilet that is just within reach of her chain.

Afterward, one of the men approaches Sally, tears off her bib overalls and the rest of her clothes, and throws her onto the mattress. Sally jumps up and starts screaming. One man strikes her on the jaw, knocking her down. Sally lays unconscious for a while.

When she wakes, she is naked and realizes the men have taken all her clothes. She is unsure of what happened and discovers the pain in her groin.

She hasn't heard the men in the trailer since yesterday and attempts to stand and look out the window. Sally tries to open the window, but it's locked and can't be budged. She hears the men returning. Discouraged, she lays down on the mattress, curls up in a ball, and tries to hide her nakedness as the men enter the room. One of the men throws her a dirty, tattered blanket, and Sally quickly covers herself. The other man walks in, throws another bag of hamburgers and a bottle of water at her, and tells her to eat. Starving, Sally quickly eats the cold, greasy food and gulps the water.

Over the last few days, the men discover that Sally is easier to handle when drunk. They don't have to fight with her to get her to cooperate while they repeatedly rape her. One man sits beside her, holding her head and forcing whiskey down her throat. She coughs and struggles against the man with the bottle, but since Sally is so small, her efforts are useless, and it doesn't take a lot of alcohol to get her drunk. The man figures he has already forced enough whiskey into her mouth, and then he drinks the remaining liquid.

Sally endured this treatment for several weeks and has mentally accepted that she will never leave this awful place. She knows her mother is in jail and her brothers are dead. Sally wonders how the men killed her brothers in their truck because Tommy is a careful driver. Why aren't the cops looking into how these guys killed her brothers? Sally is convinced that there is no one out there to help her. Now she wishes the Social Worker would check on their trailer and find her missing; maybe she could help look for her. Each day that passes, Sally loses a bit more hope that someone will help her escape the horror of her situation. She wonders how she even got into this situation. She knows the men will never let her leave because she has seen their faces, and she will never forget the faces of the ugly men.

Chapter 37

"We have to find some answers to the jockey's murders and Ed Moore's murder," Grant tells Wagner. "So far, we don't have any leads."

"First, why don't we talk to Jill Cobb about her kids? Maybe she knows something about all the trash we found on the horse trail across from the Double H ranch. She may have been involved with the robbery or knows something about it," Wagner said.

"With the trash we found, it's likely that the kids were involved. I'll set up a visitation with Mrs. Cobb at the prison, and we might get some answers."

Steele reads the report on Jill Cobb before they leave for jail. She pled guilty, and the judge considered her story of being a victim of domestic abuse and drinking when she put her boyfriend, Johnny, in the grave. Also, she managed to get sober and tried to take care of her kids before Steele arrested her. He decided to sentence her to 364 days in the county jail.

Steele and Wagner go to the jail and ask to see Mrs. Cobb. The jailer brings her into the interview room and takes off her handcuffs.

"The judge told me I would stay in the local jail so my kids could visit me. He said if he sentenced me to more than a year, I would have to go away to prison. With good behavior, he said I could get out sooner," she said, rubbing her sore wrists. "Did you bring my kids to visit?"

"That is good news about your sentence, Mrs. Cobb. We are here to ask you if you know anything about the robbery of the boarding ranch?"

"What? I didn't even know that somebody had robbed the ranch. Why would I?"

"Possibly your kids were involved?"

"My kids are good. They wouldn't rob anyone. Why are you asking all these questions?" Mrs. Cobb asks.

"I'm sorry to upset you, Mrs. Cobb. We just had to ask."

"When will I be able to visit with my kids?"

"I have some very bad news to tell you. We're sorry to tell you that your three boys died in a traffic accident yesterday. We are also looking for your daughter."

"Oh, no. My boys are all dead? What happened to them? What do you mean you are looking for Sally?" Jill said, sobbing hysterically and beating her fists on Steele's chest. "No. No, that can't be right."

"Your boys were in a vehicle accident. An eighteen-wheeler struck their vehicle, and the impact threw them from the truck because they weren't using their seat belts. The paramedics said that they didn't suffer." Steele said as he gently helped Jill to the chair.

"I can't believe it. All my boys are gone? How can this be possible?"

"Yes, ma'am, your boys died instantly. And we are looking for Sally. Your neighbor said somebody took her from the house," Steele said.

"Which neighbor? All the trailers around my house are empty. No one lives in them."

"You haven't been around for three years, and many things have changed," Steele said. "You have a neighbor, Cathy Olson, who lives about a quarter of a mile away and has been watching your children."

"Why is somebody watching my children?"

"Mrs. Olson has decided to keep an eye on your children to keep them safe because they were all alone. She is the one who

called us and described the truck and the men who took Sally. We are looking for them now."

"I've worked so hard to get sober, and I'm paying my debt for burying Johnny, but for what? All my children are gone. What do I have to live for now? I have no one."

"Please, Mrs. Cobb, you need to be strong for Sally. She will need you, and we are doing our best to find her. We have already sent an Amber alert to all television and radio stations, and the Ocala paper is keeping the public informed. The police in the area and surrounding counties are also looking for her. It is only a matter of time before we find her. When we do, we will bring her for a visit."

Steele calls the guard to take Mrs. Cobb back to her cell and tells him that her children were killed and to put her on a suicide watch.

Chapter 38

Frank Green gets up early, finally recovered from his hangover. The pain of losing his love is easing. He knows it's time to return to work. He dresses in his work clothes, goes to the barn to get hay, and takes it to the horses in the pasture. It is a beautiful spring day on May 25. Just as the sun rose over the distant trees, a gentle breeze blew the hay around as Green tossed it out of the back of his pickup. The horses approach Frank to get the fresh hay.

Three shots ring out, and the nearby workers see Frank fall while the horses scatter. The ranch hands ran to help him and call 9-1-1, telling them someone shot Frank.

Steele and Wagner are driving around town when they receive the call for help from the 9-1-1 dispatcher.

"It looks like our serial killer has struck again," Wagner said after they arrived and saw the body.

"I don't think so. Frank wasn't riding a horse and wasn't hidden by the tall trees and dense bushes on the horse trail when someone shot him. He is out here in the open when somebody shoots him. The murder looks more like a copycat killing. I wonder why anyone would want to kill Green?"

They talked to the ranch hands but didn't get any help. They were working in the barn behind Green's house or checking the fence line, and no one saw anything. They just heard the shots and saw Frank fall.

The ranch hands said the house was locked when they checked. Steele and Wagner search the area and don't find anything. Green's land has only three trees on the property, and the black wood fencing with wire mesh is around the entire pasture. He also has a fenced paddock close to the barn. The fence is intact all around the property, and there aren't any breaks.

"There isn't anything for a killer to hide behind, so the only possible way someone could have killed Green from that distance would be a sniper."

"The closest cover would be the trees and brush surrounding his property. I would guess it is about a thousand yards away. Is anyone around here with the training that could shoot that far?" Wagner asked.

"What are you talking about? What happened that far away?" Ashley Parker asks as she walks toward them.

"Will you start making some noise when you come onto a scene, so I know you're here?" Steele asks, annoyed.

"What do you have so far? Is that Frank Greene?" Ashley asks, ignoring the comment.

"Yes. It's Green, and someone has shot him three times in the back," Steele said.

"Wow. Three shots. Someone wanted to make sure he was dead."

"Good point, Parker. I wonder who had a motive to kill him and why?" Wagner asks.

"Did you say something about a thousand yards?" Parker asks.

"Since there isn't anything to hide behind, the killer must be a sniper. Can you leave out of your story that the shooter was probably a sniper? I don't want the public to know about it just yet."

"Sure, but I get an exclusive when you get ready to close his case."

"You have my word on it."

"Thanks, but everyone here is a rancher, jockey, or ranch hand. No one knows anything about being a sniper.

"Well, it looks like our work is cut out for us. I don't even know where to begin. But we better start thinking about how this happened and why," Steele said.

Chapter 39

Wagner and Steele obtained a list of all the trailers located around the area of the Cobb house. An abandoned trailer is the first one on the list. They see the front door flapping in the stiff breeze. They look into the broken windows and discover the place is deserted and wildlife has taken over the trailer. The second trailer on the list is the same, with evidence of teens using the area for drinking, hanging out, and smoking pot.

Driving to the next location, they notice the Black Dodge Ram pickup in the front yard of what appears to be another abandoned trailer. They stop before reaching the trailer and call for backup. Then, with guns drawn, Steele signals for Wagner to go into the back, and he'll enter the front door.

Steele pushes the front door open and sees a large man with long black hair pulled into a ponytail laying on top of what appears to be a child.

Enraged, Steele holsters his weapon and knocks the man off the child and starts beating him with his fists. Wagner comes in the back door and spots Steele beating someone. He runs to Steele and drags him off the man.

"Steele! Grant! Stop! Steele!! You're gonna kill him."

Steel stops hitting him and sits on the floor, rubbing his bruised and scraped knuckles, while Wagner handcuffs the beaten man.

"What are you thinking? Look, he's all bloody."

"The girl looks so tiny, and he was raping her when I came in. I can't stand pedophiles. That is why I couldn't control myself. Wagner, get a blanket or a jacket and cover the girl."

"I'll get a clean blanket from my car, and call for an ambulance," Wagner said.

"I don't need an ambulance."

"It's not for you," he said sharply. "The girl and the perp need medical care."

Several deputies arrive at the scene just before the ambulance. Thirty minutes later, the dispatcher notifies Steele that the sheriff wants to see him immediately.

"Well, that doesn't sound good," Wagner said. "Do you want me to go with you?"

"No, don't bother. I don't want to get you in trouble too. Just make sure the doctors do a rape kit on the girl."

The deputies read the Miranda warning to the perp and took him to the hospital for treatment. After being treated and released, they take him to the county jail and arrest him for kidnapping and sexual battery.

Steele isn't in a hurry. He slowly returns to the station and goes to the sheriff's office.

"Get in here and tell me what you were thinking while beating a suspect," the sheriff hollers.

"I'm not going to make any excuses. I saw the man raping a child, and I stopped him."

"I've been told the child was the nineteen-year-old Sally Cobb, who had been missing for several weeks. So, he wasn't a pedophile."

"The girl is so tiny and looks like a child. I just lost my mind and saw a large man raping a small child."

"When I hired you, you assured me that you had your anger under control and were going to anger management therapy. I guess it isn't working," the sheriff said. "I'm disappointed in you, Steele."

"The girl was so small. She looked like a child."

"You told me that you could handle your anger."

"Sorry, sir. I told you before that I despise pedophiles. They are disgusting people."

"Okay, if you want to keep your job, you will double your anger management sessions. Also, you are on administrative leave without pay for two weeks. You will be working the desk during that time," the sheriff snarls. "Now, get out of my office."

Steele slowly walks to his office with his head down.

"Was it bad?" Wagner asks after returning to the station.

"Not really. Two weeks off without pay, but I have to work the desk."

"Wow. Working the desk isn't much fun, but you can still help me work on our cases. You just can't leave the desk."

"How are the girl and the perp?"

"The girl is really messed up emotionally and physically. The hospital is doing a rape kit on her. Her name is Sally Cobb, and she was able to talk to me. She said there was another man, and they bragged about killing her brothers. The doctors will let me talk to her more tomorrow. The perp will be fine. He only has a broken nose and a black eye. The hospital treated and released him to the deputies who took him to jail."

"When you see Sally tomorrow, tell her she can visit her mother when she feels better. See if she has more information for us to help find the other guy," Steele said.

"Right. That will give Mrs. Cobb and Sally some hope."

"After I get off this desk duty, I'll interrogate the perp and learn why he kidnapped Sally."

Chapter 40

Steele gets a text from the medical examiner's Office that Green's autopsy is completed. He Facetimes their office and talks to the M.E.

"What do you have for me?" Steele asks.

"Frank Greene was five foot ten inches and weighed 190 pounds. As a rancher, he was muscular in build. There were three bullet holes in his back, one in the heart and one in each lung, which probably killed him instantly. I also sent the bullets to the forensics lab for comparison if you ever find the murder weapon. Green also had cirrhosis of the liver and was in the third stage before liver failure. He also had hepatitis B and C. Make sure you tell his wife or partner about the hepatitis B so she can be vaccinated. Hepatitis B is fifty to a hundred times more infectious than HIV."

"Thanks, Doc. Could you email a copy of your report?"

"I will send it to you when I return to my desk."

Steele visits Wagner in his office.

"I just got the autopsy report on Green, and we have a problem."

"What kind of problem do we have?"

"It appears that Greene had hepatitis B. Do we tell the Lt. Governor?"

"That is a tough one. What are you going to do about it?" Wagner asks.

"If we tell the Lt. Governor, we have to admit that we were

following Green when we didn't have a reason to do that. We can't just tell her we were nosey."

"True, but we cannot tell her. She could be infecting others if she doesn't know. We have to find a way to tell her, but how?" Wagner asks.

"Hi, guys. So, do you have some information about the kidnapping and how you managed to get on administrative leave?" Ashley asks, walking into Wagner's office. "I could use a good story now."

"All the information is in an incident report at the front desk, but right now, I have a different problem. Can you write a story about Green and say the autopsy showed he had hepatitis B?"

"I don't think I can do that without getting into trouble. Why are you so anxious to get this in the paper?"

"I'm telling you this off the record. Wagner and I were following Green, and we saw him enter the Lt. Governor's house with a bottle of wine. We need to find a way to tell her he was infected."

"You think they were fooling around? Is that why you were following him?"

"It's a long story and doesn't make any difference. So, can you help me or not?" Steele asks.

"No, I don't think I can help you, but I will keep your secret about following Green. Thanks for the information on the kidnapping. Let me know if you get any more info that I can use. Why don't you ask the sheriff what he thinks you should do about the Lt. Governor?" Ashley laughs as she leaves.

"I'm still on administrative leave for another week. Do you want to get me fired?"

"Now, what are we going to do? Aren't we obligated to inform her of the danger she is in?" Wagner asks.

"Let's just wait for now, and maybe we will think of a way to let her know."

"Well, that sounds like the easy way out."

"Do you have any bright ideas on how to handle this situation?" Steele asks.

"Right now, I don't, but I'm working on it."

Chapter 41

Steele gets a call from someone named Robert of Robert's Private Investigations, stating he has evidence from one of the killings that would interest him. Robert wants to meet with the detective to discuss his information.

Steele is curious, doesn't have any leads, and agrees to meet with the investigator at the local dive a few blocks from the station. He slips out of the station without anyone noticing since he is still on administrative leave. They decide to meet in half an hour to beat the after-work crowd.

Steele arrives early, waits a minute for his eyes to adjust to the dark and shabby interior, and secures a lonely table in the back by the neon beer signs on the wall. Just minutes later, Robert enters the establishment, dressed in an old, worn khaki trench coat tied at his ample waist with a double-knotted belt. He is a short man wearing reflective sunglasses and do-it-yourself black shoe-dyed hair crowning his pudgy white face.

Steele stands and nods to the man as he wonders how this man could be so pasty white and still live in Florida.

Robert walks toward Steele with his hand outstretched to shake hands, but Steele just sits down, ignoring his hand.

"What do you guys want to drink?" the bartender shouted behind the bar.

"Nothing for us today. So, what kind of information do you

have for me?" Steele asks Robert.

"I'm a private investigator, and a man came to me and asked me to follow his wife to see if she was unfaithful. It didn't take long to see that she was having an affair."

"Now, what does this have to do with one of the killings I'm investigating?"

"I'm a little down on my luck and was hoping there might be a reward for my information. My client hasn't paid me yet and I could use the money."

"I don't think there is a reward, but you still have to tell me who your client is and the name of his wife and the lover. By the way, do you have a valid license?" Steele asks.

"Why are you asking about my license?"

"Because if you have a valid PI's license, you wouldn't be trying to sell your information to me."

"You're right. My license expired. I didn't have the money to renew it. Is there some way I could get some money for this? It really is good. With my info, you can catch a killer."

"Okay, tell me what you have, and if it is as good as you say, I will try to find you some money."

"Colonel Theodore Eastman hired me. He wanted me to follow his wife, the Lt. Governor."

"You know you are saying a colonel had you follow his wife, the Lt. Governor? And what did you discover?"

"I know everyone from the papers and television, so I watched the Lt. Governor's house. I saw a man I identified as Frank Green enter the Eastman's house and noticed he was prepared to stay the night. I immediately contacted my client and told him. He told me to take the air out of all his tires."

"Did you do that?" Steele asks.

"No, I felt bad for the guy, so I emptied the air from one tire. I thought that would be enough."

"How does a flat tire connect the colonel to a murder?"

"I read in the papers that somebody shot Green at his ranch, and I just put two and two together. Isn't that enough info to get me a reward?" Robert asks.

"Leave me your number and let me check this out. If the information is solid, and I can make an arrest, I'll get back to you." Steele said as they left the dive.

Chapter 42

Steele is finally finished with his administrative leave and heads to the jail to question Sally's kidnapper. The jailer brought in the perp, sat him in a chair by the table, and removed the handcuffs.

"His fingerprints came back as Guy Hurtz," the jailer said.

Hurtz is rubbing his wrist, smiling, and tilting back in his chair.

Steele notices he is wearing bright blue cowboy boots, just like the neighbor told him after the abduction.

"I'm not talking to anyone, especially not you," Hurtz said. "I'm gonna sue you for breaking my nose."

"If you weren't raping that young girl, you wouldn't have a broken nose."

"She's not a young girl. She was asking for it, and I gave it to her."

"Sally is a young girl and wasn't asking for anything from you."

"All females are asking for it."

"Who was your partner? Why did you kidnap Sally Cobb?" Steele asks, slamming his hand on the table.

"I'm not telling you nothing."

"You're small potatoes. I don't want you. I want the name of the man in charge. Give me that and I'll tell the District Attorney you cooperated and get you a deal."

"If I talk, they'll kill me. Jail is better than being dead."

"The police will protect you."

"You won't be able to keep me safe. Even in jail, my boss is powerful and could have me killed anytime."

"Who is the other man who helped you kidnap the girl? Or do you want to take the rap by yourself?"

"I'm not a rat. I don't squeal on my friends."

"So, you will do the time, and your friend gets off free."

The man sits with his arms folded in front of his chest, refusing to speak with Steele. After a few minutes of silence, Hurtz finally demands an attorney.

Steele calls the guard to take him to his cell.

"He's asking for a lawyer, so I can't question him anymore. Take him back to his cell," Steel said. "I also want to talk to Jill Cobb while I'm here."

"Make yourself comfortable while I take this guy back to his cell. Then, I will bring in Mrs. Cobb from the other side of the jail. It will take a while," the guard said.

While waiting, Steele calls Wagner and gives him Guy Hurtz's name.

"Could you look up his friends, previous jail time, and the people he spent time with?"

"Sure, I'll have it ready by the time you get back here."

Thirty minutes later, the guard brings in Jill Cobb, sits her in a chair, and removes her handcuffs.

"It is nice to see you, Detective. Thank you for finding my daughter. I'm so grateful," Jill said, rubbing her wrists. "My neighbor brought her here for a visit, and we all had a long talk."

"How is Sally doing?"

"She's not well. The neighbor let her stay with her for a few days because she is too scared to stay alone. She said Sally has nightmares every night and has been throwing up a lot. The neighbor thinks it is from all the stress of someone kidnapping her and everything she went through. I'm worried about her. She has gone through a lot."

"I'll talk with the social worker and see if she can get professional help for Sally."

"That would be great. Can you talk to the Social Worker soon?"

"I'll reach out to her today and see if we can't start some kind of treatment this week."

"Thank you, Detective. I appreciate everything you are doing for us. Could you arrange for someone to bring Sally for another visit soon?"

"I'll see what I can do.

Chapter 43

After talking with Ashley and Chuck about her strange work environment at the historic hotel, Erin Kelly decided to call Steele and tell him about the unusual happenings at the hotel.

"You asked me to inform you about my suspicions of the hotel, and I think it's time to talk. When would you be available?"

"How about this evening?" Steele asks.

"That would be great. Why don't you come to my apartment, and we can have dinner with Ashley and Chuck?"

"I'm looking forward to a home-cooked meal. Would 6 p.m. be okay?" Steele asks.

"See you then."

Steele arrives holding a bottle of red wine for Erin. All four of them sit and make small talk while enjoying dinner and wine together.

"The roasted chicken dinner was delicious, and you're a fantastic cook. Now, let's get down to business. I can't wait any longer to hear about the mysterious hotel."

Erin tells Steele about the employee doors that won't open with her keys. She also mentions the housekeepers' mysterious arrival and how they drastically changed in just a few days.

"What do you mean drastic changes?"

"On Friday, I noticed the women we had working as housekeepers were gone and replaced with twenty young girls dressed in flowered skirts, blouses, and flip-flops. They were unkempt with long, dirty black hair. As I walked past, Maria, the older lady from the original group, was teaching them how to change the linens on a bed in one of the rooms."

"This is all very interesting. How long has this been going on?" Steele asks.

"The first group of twenty women was already working when I began this job in February. It was about the week before Memorial Day when the new girls showed up. That's when the afternoon manager told me to go home early on Friday and take the weekend off, which I haven't done since I started."

"How did you know about the new girls?" Steele asks.

"I walked into the breakroom and saw some of them, and the afternoon manager was talking to them. Then she saw me, and that's when she told me to leave, and take the weekend off. When I returned on Monday, the girls were all cleaned up, their hair cut short, and in hotel uniforms. And they were doing the housekeeping under the watchful eye of Maria.

"Tell Steele about hearing strange noises from the basement," Ashley said.

"That sounds interesting. What kind of sounds?"

"It could be moaning, murmuring, or whispering. I'm not sure. It's hard to describe. I just know it isn't normal. Something is going on down there, and I just can't figure it out," Erin said. "Also, several rooms on the first floor are blocked unless we need them. Then I have to ask the manager which rooms she will allow me to book."

"Well, it seems we need to make a plan to get more answers. Any idea on how you planned to do this?" Steele asks.

"Chuck has found a place in Ocala, near the hospitals, to set up his therapy shop. He is preparing everything to open soon so that we can set a wedding date, hopefully for the end of September. That would give us three months to get everything ready. That would be our excuse to see the hotel, talk to the manager about seeing the space they have for receptions, and check out the hotel rooms too. After all, we will need a place to stay before and after the wedding." Ashley said.

"Don't they have a small restaurant and bar in the back?" Steele asks.

"Yes, they do."

"Why don't you combine checking out the hotel with dinner so you can spend more time in the place?"

"That sounds great. We will ask the caterer for a sample of the food the hotel will serve at the reception. Then we can hang around longer and maybe see what's going on," Ashley said.

"That is a good idea. May I also suggest you don't acknowledge Erin? And please be careful, and don't get yourselves in trouble," Steele said.

"That may be a problem because Chuck and I went to the hotel a couple of months ago and invited Erin to dinner. So, we have already talked to her at the hotel."

"Was the manager around when you were there?" Steele asks.

"No, I don't think she was near the check-in desk then, but I can't be sure."

"Okay, just don't be friendly with Erin when you go there. Treat her like any other hotel employee, and things should be fine."

"We can do that. Chuck and I can schedule an appointment with the manager for next week. It looks like this is going to be another great story."

"Remember, Ashley, you can't print anything about the hotel until we find answers," Steele said.

"Don't worry I'm patient and can wait until the case is closed."

"Let me know what you find out. And thanks, Erin, for the delicious meal," Steele said as he left.

Chapter 44

Steele went to Wagner's office to talk about the information discovered on Guy Hurtz.

"He used to associate with a lower class of people, currently in jail. Now, he only hangs around with a guy called Michael Bowman. It seems they spent a lot of time together in jail and became good buddies when they got out. Both have a rap sheet a mile long."

"Do you have an address for him?" Steele asks.

"Sure, they both work for David Drake at the Bit of Heaven Thoroughbred Ranch."

"We can check that out later, but now, could you check on how to find a Colonel in the Army?"

"Okay. Are you planning to enlist?" Wagner asks. "I think you're too old."

"While you're at it, get the address for the Lt. Governor's Ocala's office."

"I already know that her office is near the town square."

"We can talk to the Lt. Governor and check out Drake's Ranch on the way back."

"Why this sudden interest in the Army?"

"I recently talked to an unscrupulous Private Investigator who told me about the Lt. Governor's affair with Green. The investigator was asked to check it out and reported his findings to her husband."

"So, why will we talk to the Lt. Governor?" Wagner asks.

"To find out where her husband was when someone killed Green."

"This is going to be interesting."

They arrive at the Ocala office and tell the receptionist they want to talk to the Lt. Governor, Steele said, showing her his badge and I.D.

"I'm sorry, but the Lt. Governor is busy today."

"This is very important, and we need to see her now about her husband."

"Of course, let me check," the receptionist said as she entered the large door behind her desk. A moment later, she returns with her boss.

"Gentlemen, my name is Morgan Eastman. How can I help you today?"

"My name is Detective Grant Steele, and this is CSI Jack Wagner, we are trying to reach your husband. Can you tell us where he is?" Steele asks while showing her his badge and I.D.

"I'm sorry, my husband has been out of town training his men at Camp Blanding since May 22."

"How can we reach your husband, Mrs. Eastman?"

"When he is out of town, he doesn't want anyone to contact him because he is busy. Now, if you will excuse me, I have a full schedule today," Mrs. Eastman said as she turned, walked into her office, and slammed the door.

"Does Mr. Eastman have a phone number?"

"Yes, he does, but I'm not allowed to give it to anyone. But I can tell you Camp Blanding is in Clay County, about sixty miles southwest of Jacksonville. When you get close, there will be signs pointing the way," the receptionist said.

"Thank you for your help," Steele said as he left the office with Wagner.

"Are we going there now?"

"Sure. Why not? We can get directions from the G.P.S.," Steele said while checking his phone. "Look, the Google map said it's sixty-five miles away, and we can arrive in one hour and twenty-one minutes. Let's see how accurate that time is."

"Great. I guess we're going on a road trip," Wagner said as they got into their car. "What about going to Drake's Ranch for Bowman?"

"They will still be there tomorrow. Let's get to the Colonel before he goes on deployment and leaves the country."

After an hour and thirty minutes, they arrive at Camp Blanding and check at the main gate for the colonel. The guard tells them he will be in the mess hall since it is dinner time, but they can't enter the camp without an escort. The guard checks their identification, records it on the log, makes a call, and a private arrives at the main gate with a Jeep.

"You can leave your vehicle here, and I will take you to Colonel Eastman," the private said.

They meet with Colonel Eastman and ask him where he was on the day when someone killed Green. They are impressed that he is in his mid-fifties with a short military haircut and a touch of gray at his temples. He is six feet three inches tall, standing at attention, and wearing hand-pressed field military fatigues. He would be perfect for a recruitment poster.

"Gentlemen, I have been training with my men since May 22. I have not left since then. You can ask any of the two hundred and fifty men I'm training," Colonel Eastman said in a loud, deep, booming voice.

"Why do you train at Camp Blanding when it is primarily a military reservation for the Army National Guard?"

"Camp Blanding is a joint training center, and we can use it for our training because it can accommodate three thousand military members at once. We use it often because it is convenient and fits our training needs. If you excuse me, I have to return to my dinner."

"Are you with the men constantly while you are here?"

"We do everything together, except I sleep alone in my private quarters."

"Thank you, sir, for your time. If we have any more questions, we will return."

While the escort took them back to their vehicle, Steele asked the driver to stop and asked several military personnel if they had seen the colonel in camp on May 25. Everyone said that the colonel was here on that date. Steele also asked how many entrances were on the base and discovered several ways a person could leave the camp, and no one would notice.

The escort takes Wagner and Steele back to the main gate, and they head home.

"Well, that looks like a dead end," Steele said.

Chapter 45

Steele and Wagner head to Drake's ranch on Tuesday morning.

"Hope you got some rest on Memorial Day yesterday? Today, we will be busy picking up Bowman and taking him in."

"I enjoyed my day off, but it's always good to get back to work," Wagner said.

They drive to the large Bit of Heaven Ranch and see David Drake riding his horse in the front pasture. Drake rides his horse to the fence, gets off, and walks toward the car coming down the driveway.

"Hello, gentlemen. How can I help you today?"

"We understand you have an employee named Mike Bowman. Is that correct?" Steele asks.

"Yes, he works for me. Why do you ask?"

"Do you know that he's an ex-con?"

"Sure, I believe in giving everyone a second chance, and I hire ex-cons when I feel they are deserving," Drake said.

"It is very good of you to hire convicted felons and allow them to better themselves. Did you also hire Guy Hurtz? Is Bowman here now?" Steele asks in quick succession.

"Sure, they both work for me. Bowman is probably working in the barn. I can take you there."

Steele and Wagner walk into the barn following Drake as they see Bowman running out the other door.

"Bowman. Stop. Police."

They chased him, and Wagner tackled him and handcuffed his wrists behind his back.

"Why do they always run?" Steele asks no one in particular. "Why were you running?"

"You're cops, and I run when I see cops," Bowman said. "Am I under arrest?"

"Did you have anything to do with kidnapping a young girl?"

"No, I don't do things like that. Guy Hurtz kidnapped her. I didn't have anything to do with that. Now take off the handcuffs."

"Right now, you are a suspect, and we're taking you in for a lineup."

Taking him to their car, Steele reads his Miranda warning and asks if he understands them?"

"Yeah, I understand them, alright. I've heard them often enough."

Steele radios and tells dispatch that they are bringing in Mike Bowman. He asks if they could make up a photo lineup with Bowman and Hurtz. Could they also call the Social Worker to get Sally Cobb to the station for the lineup? The Dispatcher responds that it will take a while.

"That's okay. We aren't in a hurry," Steele responds.

They arrive at the station, and Wagner takes a picture of Bowman for the lineup. After an hour, the Social Worker brought Sally Cobb to Steele's office. Sally walked in slowly with her head down and sat next to Steele on a chair that was too big for her.

"Hello, Sally. How are you today?" Steele asks gently.

"I'm okay. I talked to a doctor today, and he said I was doing better."

"She has been getting quality time with our psychologist," the Social Worker said. "He said her mental state is improving, but it will take time. But physically, she is not doing well."

"I'm sorry to hear that you aren't doing well. We'll only keep you a few minutes today, and then you can leave."

"That's okay. I don't mind."

Wagner enters the office and brings in a six-pack of photos of men who look alike and are similarly dressed.

"I want you to look at the pictures and tell me if you recognize anyone and where you saw them," Steele said, showing her the photos. Sally looks at the pictures and starts to shake uncontrollably, tears rolling down her cheeks.

"Do you know anyone?" Steele asks as he gives her his handkerchief.

"Number two and four are the men that kidnapped me and wouldn't let me go home, and they said they killed my brothers," Sally said. Steele puts his arm around Sally's shoulder to comfort her.

"Shhh, it's going to be alright." Steele said as Sally stopped sobbing.

"Thank you, Sally. You have been a big help, and Ms. Thorne will take you home now," Steele said as they left.

"Sally didn't even hesitate. She picked out Bowman and Hurtz immediately. If this ever goes to court, the District Attorney will be happy with Sally's reaction to these guys. Hopefully, she will have recovered by the time the trial starts," Wagner said.

"Hopefully, the D.A. can come up with a deal, so she won't have to face them in court. The court system is so backed up. This case won't go to trial for at least a year or more," Steele said. "But right now, we have to charge Bowman and book him in jail."

Chapter 46

Ashley calls the Ocala Manor Hotel and asks to speak to the person in charge of booking weddings in the reception room.

"Hello, my name is Brenda Boyd, and I'm the hotel's general manager. How can I help you?"

"I would like information about holding a wedding reception at your hotel."

"Of course. May I have your name and phone number?"

"My name is Ashley Parker, and my fiancé is Chuck Vaughn."

"Can I reach you at the number you are calling from?"

"Yes, that is my cell phone."

"When can you come in so I can show you our hotel and talk details?" Boyd asks.

"We are available tomorrow after lunch. Would that be okay?"

"Yes. I look forward to meeting both of you at about 1 p.m.?"

"We'll be there about one."

Chuck and Ashley are anxious about meeting the manager and hope they discover some information about the hotel. They arrive after lunch, meet the manager at the front desk, and ignore Erin.

"You must be Ashley. Welcome to the Ocala Manor Hotel. Let me show you our ballroom."

The manager unlocks the door, and they look around the large room with the same dark brown paneling as the lobby, except for four five-foot-tall white panels at the front of the room. Three brass sconce lights with Swarovski crystal are mounted on the wall between each white panel. The sconces are miniature replicas of the lobby and the ballroom chandeliers. The manager asks several questions regarding the upcoming nuptials.

Ashley tells her they are looking at an August wedding and would also like information on the catering.

"Our calendar is already booked for August. Would you consider September 9, the weekend after Labor Day?" Ms. Boyd asks as she looks at her appointment book.

"We don't have an actual date yet, so I guess September would be good. What do you think, Chuck?"

"It would give us enough time to handle all the details. Could we sample some of the food you would provide? Also, could we see one of the guest rooms?" Chuck asks.

"Let me show you a room, and then I will take you to the restaurant and order you a sample of our food," Ms. Boyd said.

They check out a room and discover a large, comfortable guest room with a king-size bed and a park view. They later wander around the lobby and the long hallway of the first floor with guest rooms on each side. They sit in overstuffed chairs in the lobby, enjoying the atmosphere of the old gas-burning fireplace in the center of a brick hearth until Ms. Boyd tells them their dinner of Chicken Marsala with mushrooms and penne pasta is ready in the restaurant. After dinner, they will have two samples of cakes to taste. The first cake will be white with lemon between the layers and creamy white frosting, and the second cake will be a decadent chocolate cake with chocolate filling and covered in dark chocolate frosting topped with chocolate shavings.

They eat in the restaurant and later enter the adjoining bar for a glass of wine and cake tasting. Chuck and Ashley have spent several hours walking around the hotel's rooms and talking with the manager.

"We would like to book a temporary date of September 9 for the ballroom and catering. We will get back to you on the number of guests and finalize the deal next week. Is that okay with you?" Chuck asks the manager.

"I can save that date for a week, and I will need a fifty percent deposit when you book. Will that give you enough time?"

"Yes, that would be perfect. I'll get back to you," Ashley said.

Chuck and Ashley leave, and both start talking at the same time.

"You go first," Chuck said.

"It was so creepy in there. Especially the ballroom. Did you see the wall sconces?"

"Sure, but what about them?"

"The brass sconce in the middle was shiny, while the other two were dull with tarnish. Didn't you see that?" Ashley asks.

"No, I just noticed how the white panels didn't match anything and looked like someone put it up as an afterthought."

"But I think I heard noises while sitting in the lobby. Did you?"

"The whole place is depressing, with all the dark paneling and maroon carpet, even with all the chandeliers. I think I also heard something in the lobby. We need to talk to Erin when she gets home. We could have stayed around the area more if she had told us where to find the basement door before we arrived," Chuck said.

"It is okay. We can call Steele when we get home and set up another meeting with him," Ashley said.

"Let's wait until Erin gets home. We can always call him tomorrow. I don't think anything is going to happen before then."

Chapter 47

Nancy Jennings texts Steele and tells him she will be there on Saturday, hoping he can spend the weekend with her. He quickly responds with an emoji smile and looks forward to seeing her.

Nancy arrives early Saturday morning, and Steele takes her for breakfast at the Go for Donuts restaurant. He orders two coffees with an apple fritter and a toasted onion bagel with cream cheese.

"So, what has been happening since we were last together?" Nancy asked as she licked the cream cheese off of her fingers.

"Did I tell you about the three boys killed in an auto accident?"

"No. How awful. What happened?"

"The brothers that we think were involved with the robbery of a horse boarding ranch died. I think the other people involved with the robbery killed them to get rid of witnesses."

"That's interesting. Why do you think the other ones were responsible for their deaths?"

"We have the word of a young girl that these guys raped. She said they told her they killed her brothers and would do the same to her if she didn't stay quiet."

"You have guys that raped a young girl, and you can prove it?"

"We can prove they raped her. We have a rape kit that proved it, and I'm sure her testimony will carry some weight at trial when she tells her story to the jury."

"I heard that you were the one that found the rapist on the young girl? How did you react?"

"Not well. The girl is petite, and I thought she was a child, so I hit the guy."

"What did the sheriff say?"

"He was furious that I hit a suspect. He didn't consider that the girl was nineteen, but she only weighed about ninety pounds and looked like a little girl."

"Well, the punishment couldn't have been too bad since you are still working."

"The sheriff doubled my anger management sessions and put me on unpaid Administrative duty for two weeks."

"Okay, what else is happening?"

"The girl's mother is in jail, and I have the Social Worker and a neighbor keeping an eye on Sally, but I'm worried about her. She isn't doing well physically."

"That sounds serious. Isn't there some way you can release the mother to care for the girl? Why don't you check with the Public Defender who had her case?"

"That is a great idea. Why didn't I think of that?"

"Well, I'm here to help if I can. Is that all that's going on?

"We also have an unscrupulous PI who claimed the wife of the colonel was having an affair. After he reported to the husband the lover's name, somebody killed the lover. We checked on the husband, who had an alibi but had a good motive, and my gut told me he was the killer. I just have to prove it."

"You have been busy since I was last here."

"You will be interested in this. It seems Erin Kelly is working in a hotel with mysterious events."

"Ooh. I like a mystery. Tell me all about it," she said excitedly.

"According to Erin, she has keys that won't open doors marked for 'employees only' and hears strange noises in the evening. So, Ashley Parker and Chuck Vaughn talked to the manager about their upcoming wedding so they could check out the hotel."

"We have to go out with Ashley, Chuck, and Erin for dinner so that I can hear all about this. And I also want to hear about their wedding," Nancy said.

"Ashley is supposed to call me and report on their visit to the hotel. We can meet with them and hear all about their findings."

"That would be great. We also have to discuss our future together when you have time because that is the main reason for my visit."

"I hope that the talk will be on a positive note."

"It's very positive."

Chapter 48

David Drake visits the Lt. Governor at her Ocala office.

"I want to see Mrs. Eastman," Drake said to the receptionist.

"I'm sorry, but she is busy all day. I can make an appointment for tomorrow if you would like."

"Tell her David Drake wants to see her now," as he walks to the large door behind the receptionist's desk.

"I'm sorry, sir, but you can't go in there," the receptionist said as she tried to stop the large man from going into Mrs. Eastman's office.

"I tried to stop him, ma'am," the receptionist said as Drake pushed past her into the office.

"It's alright," Morgan said as she closed her office door and stood before David.

"What are you doing here? Are you out of your mind? Our affair ended four months ago," she said.

"You never told me that you had the Hepatitis B virus. How many men have you been sleeping with?" Drake demands.

"What are you talking about? I don't have that," she said.

"Yes, you do. I didn't have the virus until I started sleeping with you. But now I have it. You're the only woman I've slept with."

"Are you sure you have this thing?" she asks.

"I wasn't feeling well. I was always fatigued and went to the doctor, who confirmed I had the disease. He also told me the only way to catch it is through bodily fluids, blood, or sharing needles. I don't use needles or need blood, so I had to get it from you. How many people are you sleeping with now?"

"It is none of your business who I sleep with," she says arrogantly.

"It is my business if you give me a sexually transmitted disease. You are the only one I have had sex with within the last four months. Are you sleeping with all the politicians in Tallahassee?"

"What are you talking about? Why would I tell you anything?"

"Look at this newspaper article with the Health Department announcing an alarming increase in Hepatitis B in Ocala and Tallahassee. Are you alone responsible for this outbreak? Well, you've gotta tell all those poor suckers who slept with you that they now have Hep B, which won't make them very happy."

"Leave now. I don't feel very well," Morgan said. "Just get out."

"Of course, you don't feel well. You have Hep B, and you have to go to a doctor so you can get treatment," Drake said, wiping the tears off her cheek and putting his arms around her. "Why are you so loveable? After all, you have done to me. I still love you."

"How did that get in the paper?" she asks.

"The reporter explains the increased number of cases reported to the Health Department recently, and they want to tell the people so they can protect themselves."

"What am I going to do? This disease will ruin my career."

"Shouldn't you be more worried about all the men you've infected than your lousy career? I'm disappointed in you and thought you were a better person than this. Why can't you do the right thing?"

"I don't know. What is the right thing?"

"The Health Department said that if the man used protection, he wouldn't get the disease. The paper also reported that anyone with the condition should go to the Health Department. They will help notify anyone you recently slept with that you may have infected.

"I can't do that. I'm scared," Morgan said.

"Don't worry. I will go with you and support you."

"What about your wife?"

"I told you a long time ago that my wife and I no longer love each other, and this will be my opportunity to get a divorce."

"Oh, David, will you help me with this?"

"You know I will. Can you get away for a few hours and meet me at the hotel?"

"Just make sure you have protection."

"Don't worry, I will definitely have protection."

Chapter 49

Steele gets a call from Private Jensen at Camp Blanding, and he tells him that the colonel doesn't have an alibi for May 25, and he can prove it. Steele tells him that he will be there in two hours.

Wagner asks where Steele is going in such a hurry.

"First, I have to get a warrant, and then I'm returning to Camp Blanding. Do you want to come along?"

"Sure, why are we taking another road trip?"

"It seems my gut was right, and the colonel doesn't have an alibi for the shooting of Frank Green, and we are going to the camp to hear all about it."

"First, we'll check on the time it takes to get to Camp Blanding, going just above the speed limit. Not fast enough to get caught, just enough to get there quickly."

"This is going to be very interesting."

They arrived at Camp Blanding in about one hour.

"That's better than the first time we came here. You weren't really going that fast. Just about eight miles over the speed limit."

They arrived at the entrance and asked to see Private Jensen.

"He is in the infirmary, and I will get someone to take you there," the guard said.

An escort arrived at the gate, taking Steele and Wagner to the infirmary. They entered and talked to Jensen.

"Nice to meet you, Private," Steele said, shaking hands with him.

"Now, how can you break the colonel's alibi?"

"First, sit for a minute and just listen," Jensen said.

Wagner and Steele sit and look at each other with a puzzled look. There is a loud voice booming outside, which they easily heard inside.

"Did you hear that voice?" Jensen asks.

"Yes, it is deafening. Who is that?" Steele asks.

"That is the colonel barking orders. He does this constantly when outside training. He only stops for lunch and dinner. Otherwise, he is very loud."

"Okay, I understand, but how does this affect his alibi?"

"On May 25, my first day in sick bay after I broke my ankle, I didn't hear from the colonel until after lunch. So, he wasn't here in the morning, or I would have heard him."

"Why are you in sick bay private?"

"I broke my ankle during training because the colonel insisted that we all run through the woods instead of walking, and I stepped in a gopher hole and broke my ankle."

"So, basically, you have a grudge against the colonel. Is that why you're telling us this story?"

"Sure, I'm mad my training is on hold because of my broken ankle. I'm telling you because it's all true. Also, check with the cooks. The colonel never misses a meal, and cooks will tell you he wasn't here the morning of the 25th."

"Okay. Are you willing to testify to that in court?"

"Of course, it's the truth."

"Thanks, Jensen. We'll check this out on our way out of here."

Steele and Wagner leave and ask their escort to take them to the mess hall. After thoroughly questioning the mess hall staff, he finally gets the correct answers, and they go outside.

They ask the escort to take them to the colonel.

"Good afternoon, Colonel Eastman. We are here to arrest you for the murder of Frank Green."

While Steele read him his Miranda Rights, Wagner cuffed the colonel's hands behind him."

"You don't have any authority here. You are on military property, and you can't arrest me," the colonel bellowed. "You can't prove anything."

"On May 25, you left the camp before sunrise, drove to Ocala, staked out Green's ranch, and shot him. We also learned you are a trained sniper and received medals for your expert shooting. You could return to camp in a little over two hours. The only problem was that you missed breakfast and didn't count on the kitchen staff noticing your absence. Private take us to the Colonel's sleeping quarters."

"What are you going to do there?"

"We are going to search your room."

"You can't do that without a warrant."

Steele takes the paper from his jacket pocket and gives it to the general. "But we do have a warrant."

The men entered his room, searched the colonel's foot locker, and discovered a Savage Arms Axis bolt-action rifle disassembled with ammunition.

"I'm sure this will match the bullets removed from Green," Steele said as Wagner put the rifle in an evidence bag.

They loaded the colonel in the jeep, the escort took them to their vehicle, and Steele drove to the Ocala jail and booked him.

"I'll be out before dinner. You don't know who you are dealing with."

"I wouldn't be too sure about eating your dinner at the camp tonight."

As they left the jail, they returned to their offices. Ashley Parker greeted them in the hallway.

"What have you been up to today?" Ashley asks.

"Your timing is perfect. We just booked Colonel Theodore Eastman on charges of murder for killing Frank Green."

"You've got to be kidding. Give me all the details. This is going to be a great story," Ashley said.

Steele gives Ashley all the facts of the case as she writes everything in her reporter's notebook.

"Thanks, Steele," she said as she left.

Chapter 50

Steele called Nancy at her hotel and asked if she could stay in town for a few more days because he had taken emergency time off from work to travel to Georgia and wanted her to go along.

"Of course, I have a lot of vacation time. I will have to let the office know I'm taking more time, but where are we going?"

"I have a Marine buddy in Helen, Georgia, who is dying and wants to see me because he wants a favor," Steele said as they checked Nancy out of her hotel and headed North. "His name is Duncan White, and everyone called him Whitey because of his name. His hair was completely white when he was a young man in the Marines with me. He saved my life. I owe this guy."

"Of course, Grant, and while driving, maybe we can talk about our future together?" Nancy asks.

"Okay, you go first. You will have plenty of time since it will take about eight hours to get there."

"Where is this Helen, Georgia? I've never heard of it."

"It is in North Georgia, just south of North Carolina. It's beautiful up there. I'm sure you will enjoy it."

"Oh, I'm sure I will. What else can you tell me about Whitey?"

"He is a few years older than me, and we served four years together in the Marines. We both got honorable discharges, and I went to Las Vegas, and he just kept moving around until he ended up in Helen. We always kept in touch and have gotten together several times. He is a good guy, and I would do anything for him."

As they drove, Nancy said she considered retiring and moving to Marion County.

"I have worked long enough to get a nice pension, and I've saved a lot of money while caring for my mother all these years," she said. "What do you think of that idea?

"That sounds like a great idea. I would like you to live closer to me. But you can't be old enough to retire. You would be bored with nothing to do," Steele said.

Nancy explains that she is already forty-six years old and has worked in the Communication department since she graduated from high school at eighteen.

"Over the years, I have received many promotions, giving me more money and responsibilities. So, I've cared for my ailing mother since 2001 until she died in 2020, I didn't have time to do anything,"

Nancy said. "I think I'm ready for a very long vacation."

"You have a point there. I didn't realize you had to take care of your mother. Why didn't you say anything?" Steele asked.

"Because I'm a private person and didn't like discussing my problems with others."

They continue talking about everything as the miles quickly pass.

"Okay, we are almost there, but first, let's check into the Country Inn & Suites and unpack before we go looking for Whitey."

"Everything is so cute here. All the houses and stores look like an authentic German town."

As Steele checked into the hotel, while Nancy went to the bathroom.

"Would you believe they upgraded us to a room with a real fireplace?" Steele asks as Nancy joins him, and they head to the elevator.

"Oh, that's wonderful. I love fireplaces."

They went to room 300 and saw a large king-sized bed with a stone gas fireplace next to the window with a view of tall trees.

"This is wonderful, Grant. Since it is the end of August let's turn on the A/C on high so we can enjoy the fire later while lying in the large bed."

"Sure, that will be nice. Now, let's find some food and visit Whitey."

After they enjoyed a plate of Schnitzel covered with a cream sauce, bratwurst, and sauerkraut with a Hofbrau original beer, they drove north for twenty miles on steep, winding mountainous roads.

"Why do you have a white knuckle hold on your seat belt?" Steele asks.

"Well, you are going pretty fast. The narrow road doesn't have a shoulder, and there is a sharp drop off the side of this mountain."

"Okay. I'll slow down. Just relax."

He continued the drive to the little town of Clayton, and the GPS showed the way to the private Hospice home. The nurse opened the door and told them that her patient was very ill and that he probably wouldn't last much longer. She then took them to Whitey's bed.

"Thanks for coming, Grant," Whitey said in a faint whisper.

Grant looks at a gaunt, frail-looking man lying on a hospital bed. His eyes are sunken, his head is bald, and his face is wrinkled.

"You haven't changed a bit," Steele said with a smile.

"I see you still know how to lie to me."

"This is my fiancé, Nancy Jennings. I wanted you to meet her."

"Pleased to meet you, Nancy. It's about time you found yourself a nice girl," Whitey said, gasping for air.

"Now, tell me the favor that you want."

"I want you, Grant, to find my daughter, Summer Smythe. She disappeared in October2021."

"Did you report her missing?"

"Of course, I did. And I hired a PI, but my money ran out before he found anything. She was supposed to attend a school in the Marion County area of Florida, and I haven't heard from her in two years."

"I can look into it, Whitely, but maybe she just left with her boyfriend."

The old man continued after a coughing spell that left him short of breath. "Summer had a future. She was only nineteen years old. She had a four-year degree scholarship and didn't have a boyfriend," Whitey said, gasping for air. "The cop said he found her car in the parking lot where she worked but nothing else. I don't believe the cop. I know she's gone and needs a proper funeral. Will you find her and give her a nice funeral?"

"Is she your biological daughter?"

"Yes," he whispered.

"Why didn't she have your last name?

"She didn't like her last name because everyone called us Whitey, and she didn't want to endure the same torture all her life as I did, so she legally took her mother's maiden name when she started high school."

"I will do my best to find her. But I'm in the middle of a serial killing in Ocala that I must solve first. As soon as it is over, I will find her. I promise you."

"I understand. My daughter has been missing for two years. I don't think a few more months will make any difference. I trust you, Grant. If anyone can find her, I know it's you."

"Sure, Whitey, but your nurse said you didn't have much time left."

"I just needed to see you and ask you this favor before I died. Now, I can die in peace. Thanks, my friend."

The men hug. Then Steele and Nancy drove back to their hotel in Helen where he received a call saying Duncan White had died.

"I'm sorry your friend is gone," Nancy said as she touched his shoulder.

"At least I said goodbye to him," Steele said with a frown.

They stayed the night, enjoyed the fireplace, and headed back home early in the morning.

Chapter 51

After returning from Georgia, Steele took Nancy to book a room at the Comfort Inn & Suites Hotel. They got her settled and then met with Erin, Ashley, and Chuck.

"Tell me everything you discovered at the hotel," Steele said.

"There is something mysterious about the ballroom," Ashley said.

"We both heard unusual noises at the hotel," Chuck said.

"This is so interesting. Can I go and see this hotel?" Nancy asks. "Also, tell me all about the wedding."

"We don't have any plans yet. We just used it as a story that Chuck and I will get married on September 9 so we could check out the hotel," Ashley said. "We probably will be setting a wedding date soon, but we will not be using that hotel."

"I gave this info about the new housekeeping staff to the FBI Tampa Field Office before we went to Georgia, and they have been conducting a human trafficking sting around the hotel, but I haven't heard anything about it since we just got home," Steele said.

"What do you mean 'human trafficking sting'?" Ashley asks.

"Now, you can't write about this until we have some answers and possibly arrests. Do you understand?" Steele asks Ashley.

"I'll keep all this to myself if you give me your word that I'll get the scoop when it's all over."

"You know I'll give you an exclusive on this case when it's finished."

"Okay. Give us an update," Ashley said.

"When you told me about the young girls starting as new housekeeping personnel, I informed the FBI, Special Agent in Charge, and they set up a sting. We should get more information soon."

"Did you read my story on the illegal horse meat market?"

"No. What's it all about?"

"I wrote that The Epoch Times based in New York City recently reported that Ocala has the unfortunate new title as the epicenter of the illegal horse-meat market in the country. I also found that the Marion County Sheriff's Department has handled three horse slaughter cases in the past five years. Maybe you should check their closed cases to learn more about them."

"How did you get that information?"

"Simple. I just used my Press Pass and the Freedom of Information Act; they gave me the information. Maybe you should try it."

"What else did you find out?" Steele asked.

"The founder of the Animal Recovery Mission, Richard Cuoto, reported in the paper that hundreds of illegal slaughterhouses operate throughout Florida, especially in Miami. Now, isn't that interesting?"

"How did you find Cuoto?"

"Simple, it was in the sheriff's reports, and I emailed him. He was happy I was writing another article to inform people about this horrible practice."

Steele's phone rang, interrupting the conversation.

"Sorry, I have to take this."

After listening for a minute, Steele said. "Okay, I'll be there in twenty minutes."

"I have an emergency. Nancy, can I leave you here until I get back?"

"Don't worry. I'm sure Ashley or Erin can give me a ride back to my hotel," Nancy said.

"Good. I don't know how long I'll be."

Chapter 52

Steele arrived at the hospital to meet with Wagner.

"What's going on?"

"Sally Cobb's neighbor, Cathy Olson, called the ambulance, and the paramedics took her to the hospital. She is in critical condition, and the doctors are working on her."

"I was worried and checked on Sally since I hadn't seen her outside all day. I found her on the floor with a lot of blood and called the paramedics," Mrs. Olson explained to Steele.

They all sat down and waited for word about Sally. After several long hours in the waiting room, the emergency room doctor slowly approached the group.

"I'm sorry, but Sally wasn't strong or healthy enough to handle the pregnancy. She had a miscarriage, and we couldn't control the bleeding."

"I didn't even know she was pregnant," Olson said.

"It's a shame, she was so young and had survived a horrible tragedy," Steel said, putting his head in his hands. "I guess the whole ordeal was too much for her."

"The poor thing didn't have a chance. There isn't anything I can do here, so I'm gonna go home and have a good cry," Olson said.

Steele and Wagner return to their offices, call the Marion County Department of Children and Families, and ask to speak to Social Worker Thorne. The person on the phone tells him that Mrs.

Thorne is no longer with the department. Steele requested to talk to the manager.

"I'm sorry I can't give you any information on an ongoing investigation involving Mrs. Thorne," the manager said.

"I'm Detective Grant Steele with the Marion County Sheriff's Office, and I've been working with her. Can't you tell me anything?"

"I'm sorry, but you have to talk to the fraud division to get any more information."

Steele checked with the Fraud detectives to find Beverly Thorne is in jail and charged with money fraud.

"When did this happen?" Steele asks the fraud detective working the case.

"Just recently, we have found evidence that she was taking half the money given to foster parents for the children in their care because she fraudulently increased the number of children in their home for more money. Mrs. Thorne also received all the money sent for the care and supervision of the Cobb family. We have reports that she did this for at least two years. I don't have any other information to give you," the fraud detective said. "I'm surprised she got away with this deception for so long.

"Thanks for the info. I appreciate you telling me."

Steele contacts the Department of Children and Families and tells them that Sally Cob died, and they wouldn't have to visit her anymore.

The manager explained that being a Social Worker is hard work. They have to visit and report on the progress of all their cases monthly. This type of work has a lot of burnout; not everyone can handle the workload, but some are especially good with children.

"It seems that Ms. Thorne was taking money by fraudulently increasing the number of children in the foster homes so the parents would get more money, and she took half," Steele told Wagner after he closed his phone.

"She did look worn out, but I didn't think she was into stealing from the government," Wagner said.

"She certainly didn't spend the money on herself or her vehicle. I wonder what she did with the money?"

The report said one of her foster parents had a guilty conscience and called the cops.

She pled not guilty and is out of jail on a bond until the court schedules a trial.

Ashley goes to Steele's office.

"I just got the police report about Beverly Thorne. Why didn't you tell me about her?"

"We just found out about this ourselves. Did you know that Sally Cobb just died?"

"Isn't that the girl that I wrote about that was kidnapped and raped? How did she die?"

"She was pregnant and had a miscarriage and by the time she was taken to the hospital the doctors couldn't control the bleeding."

"That's too bad, but it will make a great story. Thanks for the info."

Chapter 53

A week after Steele returned from Georgia, the FBI called Steele to report on the human trafficking sting at the Ocala Manor Hotel.

They've watched the hotel for a week and found several men leaving through the back and front doors on different evenings and at unusual hours.

"We didn't have probable cause to arrest them, so we got their names and addresses and had to let them go. They all claimed to be enjoying a drink at the bar and left, and we couldn't prove otherwise. We are trying to get an undercover agent in there for more information," the FBI agent said. "Do you think your informant would be of any help to us?"

"I don't think that would be a good idea. She keeps her eyes open, but the keys they gave her don't open the locked doors. You need someone to get a position with the hotel to get past those locked doors," Steele said. "I think the locked doors hold the answer."

The FBI agent also explains that human traffickers prey on members of marginalized communities and vulnerable individuals, especially children in the welfare system or children who have been in the juvenile system. Most victims come from Latin America, Columbia, Cuba, Peru, or Nicaragua and usually only speak Spanish. The traffickers prey on people hoping for a better life. The people manage to obtain enough money to help them cross borders. The traffickers pick up the families and give them false promises of a better life, but they are separated and told they must work to pay off their debt to be together again. The female victims are usually forced into sex trafficking until they pay off their debt, which never happens.

"So, you can see why we need to get hard proof of sex trafficking and forced labor to solve this case. We also need probable cause to get a warrant to search the hotel."

"Any idea on how we can get the probable cause?" Steele asks.

"We are working on it, but don't have the answer yet." The FBI Agent said.

After a search of the agents' backgrounds, they discovered no one had the qualifications of another profession that could work at the hotel and get into the locked rooms. Instead, the FBI found two agents who spoke perfect English and Spanish. Then, put them undercover in the hotel to get information on the housekeepers or find a way to open up some of the locked doors that Erin couldn't open. The man in charge selected Special Agents Santos Garcia and Josephina Santiago to go undercover at the hotel. The two agents agreed to go as a married couple and rent a room for two days to obtain the needed information.

After checking in the first day, Santos called the front desk, complained that they didn't have enough towels, and requested they send more towels to their room. One of the housekeepers knocked on their door with the towels.

"Please put the towels into the bathroom," Garcia said in perfect Spanish."

"Have you been working here very long?" he asked after the young girl put the towels away.

"No, señor. I will only work here until I pay off my debt," the housekeeper said in Spanish.

"You are so young. What kind of debt could you have?" Garcia asks.

"I must not talk with you. The lady in charge will be angry with me. She told us not to talk to anyone."

"Then go. I don't want to get you in trouble. Thank you for the towels."

The undercover Agent texts headquarters with the information he received from the housekeeper.

"Is this enough to get a warrant, or do we need more probable cause?"

"It is a start, but we better get more information on what is happening in the hotel. Can you get that?"

"We will do our best. We still have another day here,"

Chapter 54

Wagner and Steele are reviewing the evidence to find the killers of the jockeys and Edward Moore when the phone rings. The 9-1-1 dispatcher tells Steele that the fire department is putting out a fire at the Cobb trailer, and the Fire Chief wants Steele there.

"Come on, Wagner, we're going to a fire," Steele said, grabbing his jacket from his chair and heading to the car.

Arriving at the Cobb's trailer, the fire department finished putting out the fire and stored their equipment.

"Glad you were able to get here before we left," the Fire Chief said. "There is no doubt that the fire is the work of arsonists, and I know this trailer is part of your case."

"Was anyone hurt?"

"No. The trailer was empty. Somebody started the fire by pouring gasoline around the back of the building and lit it with a match. The trailer was old and went up quickly," the Fire Chief said. "They blew out the match and threw it away from the fire. I don't know why people do that."

The neighbor, Cathy Olson, walks to the burnt trailer while Steele talks to the Fire Chief.

"Thanks, Chief. We will take it from here. This is Mrs. Olson, the neighbor that kept an eye on Sally, the former resident."

"There is nothing left," she said. "Good thing Sally wasn't here."

"It seems someone started the fire, but the trailer was engulfed before the fire department could put it out," Steele said. "How do you always see the traffic going by around here?"

"I have a desk by the front window and enjoy playing Solitaire. I always look at everything happening here because I like to know what's going on."

"Well, I'm happy that you are a busybody, or we wouldn't have known that someone had kidnapped Sally," Steele said. "You have been very helpful to us."

"I saw the same black truck that took Sally drive slowly past my house just a few minutes ago. I watched them get out and go to the rear of the trailer. When I saw the fire, I called 9-1-1," Cathy said. "They looked like the same men that kidnapped Sally. Do you think they thought Sally was in the trailer when they set it on fire?"

"They're supposed to be in jail. They couldn't have set the fire," Steele said.

Steele asks Wagner to check the computer to see if Bowman and Hurtz are still in jail.

"The records show they were released on bail two days ago," Wagner said after checking his computer.

"Who paid their bail?"

"The records indicate that David Drake posted their bond."

Ashley arrives as the Fire Chief and his crew leave.

"What happened here?" she asks.

"Someone set fire to the Cobb trailer. No one was hurt, and you can get more information from the Fire Chief."

Ashley talks to Mrs. Olson then drives to see the Fire Chief to get his information about the fire.

Upset, Steele and Wagner thank Mrs. Olson for her help and drive out to Drake's ranch. They see Bowman and Hurtz by the bunkhouse as they go down the winding driveway to the Bit of Heaven Thoroughbred Ranch's main house.

Drake rides his horse to the driveway to meet Steele and Wagner.

"How can I help you today?" he asked as he got off his horse.

"Why did you bail out your guys?" Steele asks.

"They're my ranch hands, and I needed them to do their work, so I bailed them out."

"Where were they three hours ago?"

"Here working."

"Did you see them?" Steele asks.

"Of course. What are you trying to pin on my boys now?"

Hurtz and Bowman walk toward the men in the driveway. When they get close, Steele notices the men smell of smoke.

"Why do your men smell like smoke? Were they at the Cobb trailer setting it on fire?"

"No, they were burning brush in the fire pit. Now, that's enough. You can stop harassing my men and leave us all alone," Drake demanded.

"Just make sure they are around for the trial," Steele said.

"My lawyer said you don't have much of a case since your main witness is no longer available to testify, according to the newspaper."

"I wouldn't count on that. We may have a surprise witness.

Chapter 55

Ashley and Chuck decided to have their wedding on Saturday, September 30, which gave them time to make all the arrangements for a small, personal wedding with close friends.

Erin has called Nancy and invited her to go dress shopping with Ashley. Nancy arrives on August 31, booked a room at the Dunnellon hotel, and then drives to Ashley's apartment.

They all climb into Erin's vehicle and go to a bridal shop in Ocala.

"I know it will be a small wedding, but I just turned thirty-five, and I've never been married. I've dreamed of the perfect wedding gown since I was a little girl. I know wedding gowns are very expensive, and I'm willing to pay a ridiculous amount for my wedding dress since I've finally found my soulmate."

The store clerk brings Ashley numerous dresses and assists her in putting them on. After trying eight dresses, the girls made a decision.

"They are all beautiful dresses, but I liked you in the V-shaped waistline that balloons with yards and yards of tulle from the waist down with the jeweled neckline and the floral lace appliques along the bodice," Nancy said. "It accentuates your great figure."

"I agree. That is the perfect dress for you, Ashley. The cathedral train gives the dress the finishing touch," Erin said. "Try it on again so we can be sure."

"The clerk helps Ashley put the dress on.

"I do feel like a princess in this dress. So, I guess this is the one I'm picking. And the price is something in my budget."

The store clerk puts a tiara attached to a lace veil on Ashley's head while she's still wearing the dress.

"Oh. That is perfect. The veil and dress are beautiful together," Erin said.

After the clerk takes measurements for the gown alterations, Ashley and the girls go for a drink at a Sports Bar and discuss the rest of their plans.

"Erin is my Maid of Honor, but I would also like you also to be in the wedding party, Nancy."

"I would be honored to be your bridesmaid. What should I wear?"

"I don't want you to have to buy a bridesmaid dress, so you and Erin can just wear a nice dress. I hope that is okay with you?"

"That would be great," Nancy said.

"Have you picked out the colors for your wedding?" Erin asked.

"I went to the florist and picked out moss green and coral carnations with baby's breath for my bouquet. The bridesmaids will have a smaller bouquet to carry. And the groomsmen will have carnation boutonnières."

"That will be great. We can find our bridesmaid's dress to match your color theme," Nancy said.

"Since the wedding will be very small, I don't think we need invitations. Chuck's parents are coming here from New York two days before the wedding, giving me a chance to get to know them a little. Unfortunately, my dad passed away a couple of years ago, but my mother will be able to attend. We also invited Jack Wagner since I feel he is part of the family."

"That is wonderful. I'm so excited," Erin said.

"I'm glad you chose that special wedding dress and veil. You look elegant in it and deserve to be glamorous on your special day," Nancy said.

"Since we've finished all our errands, I'll call Grant to pick me up. We have reservations for dinner tonight. I know you and Chuck have plans to check on the venue for the wedding and reception."

"That will be fine. We have already made a down payment on a small room at the World Equestrian Center. We are just going there tonight to pick out our menu and make the final decisions, and Erin will help us."

Grant picks up Nancy at the bar and heads back to his home to make her a home-cooked meal.

"I thought we had reservations for tonight."

"We do. The reservations are at my home. I'm cooking for you," he said as they went to his apartment.

"You're kidding. I'm surprised you even know how to do grocery shopping, let alone cook a meal. I'm impressed. I hope it tastes good."

"I've been practicing, so I hope it turns out okay. Why don't you sit on the couch until dinner is ready, and I'll bring you a glass of wine?"

After much preparation, pots and pans clashing, dinner is finally ready to serve. Nancy is escorted to the small table and sees a lovely, decorated table with flickering candles and two steaming plates of spaghetti and meatballs.

"Oh, Grant. It's lovely and smells delicious. Let's eat."

After stuffing themselves with the spaghetti and warm garlic bread, they retreat to the couch with their wine.

"That was so good. Let me do the dishes and clean up the kitchen."

"No, I'll do that tomorrow. Right now, we'll enjoy some quiet and alone time together."

"It's about time we had some quality time together. That's fine with me," she said dreamily.

Chapter 56

Paula Drake and Helen Lane go to their favorite posh golf course restaurant for their fifteenth-of-the-month lunch in September.

José, the waiter, greets them at the door.

"Welcome. It is always a pleasure to serve you. Would you like a glass of Chardonnay?" José, the waiter, asks as he escorts the women to their reserved table overlooking the golf course and holds their chair, each in turn.

"Yes, José, that would be wonderful. What is the special for today?" Paula asks as she flirts with the handsome waiter.

"Today, our special is garlic shrimp with roasted Parmesan asparagus."

"That would be wonderful, José. Helen, is that okay with you too?"

"That sounds delicious."

"Excellent choice. I will put in your order and bring your wine right over."

"Have you heard all the excitement that is going on?" Paula asks Helen as José places the glasses of wine on the table.

"No, what are you talking about?"

"Ashley Parker is getting married, and the wedding is two weeks from Saturday at WEC."

"How did you find out about the wedding?" Helen asks.

"It's all over Facebook, and she put an engagement announcement in the paper."

"You know I don't waste my time on Facebook. So, tell me what you read about the wedding."

"The announcement said the wedding will be a small private affair at WEC. Also, Laura is out and about and spends a lot of time at WEC watching the fall equestrian events. She acts like she was never sick," Paula said. "I also heard she is entering the dressage Freestyle competition. Can you believe it?"

"Now, Paula, she is young and lucky to have bounced back from her ailments," Helen said.

"Of course, you would say that. By the way, how is your daughter Cat doing?"

"We are so pleased. Cat is doing great and finally has her kidney problems under control."

"José, I would like another glass of wine, please."

"Yes, Mrs. Drake. I will get it for you. Mrs. Lane, would you also like another?"

"No, thank you. I'm fine."

After the waiter leaves, Helen asks. "Are you okay? You usually only have two glasses of wine throughout lunch, but you're ordering a second glass, and José hasn't even served the food yet."

"I need wine to help me relax. David is angry and upsetting me because he couldn't find an experienced jockey to race his thoroughbred horse in the Derby. He knows his horse would win since someone stole Edward Moore's horse, leaving him with the only horse in the area trained and qualified to compete and win."

"Don't worry about that. Your husband can always try again next year."

"Come on, Helen, you know a thoroughbred only has one year to try and win the Derby. Only a three-year-old can compete in that race."

"You're right, but with Howard having dementia, he doesn't

talk too much, and we don't have a horse to be concerned about the Derby."

"David is also very moody and grumpy because Detective Steele arrested and charged two of his ranch hands with kidnapping a young girl. He had to bail them out of jail."

"Oh, my. Is it true?" Helen asked.

"Of course, it isn't true. David would never have criminals working around the ranch with my mother living there too. I'm sure it is all a big mistake, and he'll have his lawyer straighten it out."

The waiter brings the plates of food to the women while Paula asks for another glass of wine.

"Paula, are you sure you want a third glass of wine? Will you be able to drive home?"

"Don't worry about me. I can take care of myself. I just need something to calm my nerves. David has been unbearable for the last few months, and I need some wine to help me cope.

Chapter 57

Steele and Wagner have spread out all the evidence on the table to compare each of the murders.

"The first murder was last November, and we still don't know the person or persons that committed these crimes. It is almost a year, and we still don't have anything," Steele said. "What are we missing?"

The men go over the evidence, looking for similarities.

The first two victims, Jimmy Sparks and Kyle Adams, were retired jockeys from the Black House of Dominoes owned by Edward Moore.

"Adams had a broken neck, and it looked like an accident until we found Sparks. The evidence of a firecracker showed that it wasn't an accident. Sparks received the head wound when he hit his head on the rock after falling off his horse, and he also had broken bones," Wagner said.

"The pictures you took of Adams showed his broken neck. The close-up of Sparks shows the bloody rock he hit when he landed. They must be related because it can't be a coincidence how they both died. One jockey dying in that way, but not two."

Willie Flynn was the third victim, but someone shot him at close range. He was Frank Green's jockey from the Green Oaks Ranch. Somebody shot Mr. Moore while he was riding his horse.

They were all killed while on the horse trail. However, Green's shooting was on his land, not the trail.

"We have proof that the Colonel shot Frank Green to make it look like a copycat killing. We can thank Robert of Robert's Investigations for giving us the information to close that case and send it to the District Attorney."

They continue to look over the evidence collected from the other crimes.

"None of this makes sense. The evidence showed that somebody murdered the three Cobb brothers. Why?"

"My gut tells me that all these cases are connected. I just don't know how right now. Somebody stole the Lane horses after it appeared the boys were stalking the place. They were working with some adults because I don't believe the boys were smart enough to pull off that job by themselves. They wouldn't know how to get rid of all the horses that were stolen or the horses missing from the murders on the trail," Steele said, rubbing his hand through his hair. "What happened to all the horses? Moore's thoroughbred was an expensive horse. Why was he taken?"

"You're right. Also, why did the boys have to die? Why was Sally kidnapped but kept alive? We just have to find the connection to all of this."

"What are we missing? Let me have the pictures of the scenes."

Wagner moves all the pictures to another table and spreads them around putting them in order of the deaths. Carefully scanning the photos, Steele notices something.

"Do you have a magnifying glass?"

"Sure," Wagner said, handing him the magnifying glass from his desk. "What do you see?"

"Look. At the edge of the trampled grass. Doesn't that look like a piece of metal or something that shouldn't be there?"

"You're right."

"Okay, let's go back to the scene. Maybe it's still there."

They return to the scene with a rake and the picture in hand.

Wagner rakes the ground that matches the picture and digs up mulch, roots, and dirt, but nothing metal or unusual.

"Nothing is turning up. Maybe we should move down the trail a bit and try again. This place also looks like the photo."

"Okay. Let me have the rake for a while."

The men take turns raking around the trail until they finally find the piece of metal, caked with months of dirt and horse manure.

"We never would have found this if it wasn't for the picture. Look. It's a coin from one of the ranches. Let's take it back to the lab and clean it to see which ranch it's from."

They return it to the lab and prepare it for cleaning. Wagner sets out a plate, puts in the piece of metal, and pours apple cider vinegar on it. They wait five to ten minutes. Wagner uses a soft bristle brush on the coin, rinses and dries it.

"Look. It's a coin from the Drake ranch. One of their ranch hands probably dropped it," Wagner said.

"We don't have any idea who had the coin, so we can't prove who the person was that dropped it. That would be circumstantial evidence and hard to prove," Steele said." But it's a start. Maybe we will solve this case after all."

Chapter 58

The weeks slowly pass for the nervous bride and groom. John and Barbara Vaughn arrive on Thursday before the wedding. Everyone gets together and goes to Olive Garden for dinner and an opportunity to get acquainted.

Barbara embarrasses Chuck by showing his baby pictures and telling everyone all the lovable things he did as a youngster.

"You will have to excuse my wife. She had been waiting for this day for years and insisted on bringing all his baby books on the plane to show his bride. We had to pay to check the bags and then pay an expensive overweight charge on her suitcase because of all the books."

"Please, Mom, put the baby books away until later. It's embarrassing."

"No, I want to see how cute you were as a baby," Ashley said.

Ashley and Chuck's mother enjoyed looking at pages and pages of pictures of Chuck's early years.

"You were an adorable baby, Chuck. Our children will be beautiful."

The evening quickly comes to a close, and everyone heads out of the restaurant and heads off to their beds.

After breakfast at John and Barbara's hotel, Chuck and Ashley spent the day confirming that all the arrangements for the next day were ready.

The group plans to meet for a quick dinner at the World Equestrian Center's Yellow Pony Pub and Garden. Everyone is too excited to eat a big dinner. The group checks the room's location for the next day's nuptials. Ashley is staying in the hotel's bridal suite so the girls can return in the morning to help her dress. Everyone goes home. Ashley and Chuck embrace and kiss before he leaves. Ashley ensures that Chuck stays at his place until just before the wedding, so he won't see the bride until she walks down the aisle. He reluctantly agrees.

Saturday arrives, and Erin and Nancy are helping Ashley with her hair and makeup before assisting her with the bridal dress. There is a lot of excitement as the ladies care for the bride.

John, Barbara, and Ashley's mom go to the bridal suite to see Ashley and wish her every happiness.

"My, but you look beautiful, Ashley," John said.

"He is right. You and the dress are gorgeous," Ashley's mom said. "And your bridesmaid's dresses almost match the coral in your flowers."

"Nancy and I went shopping together and found matching dresses for this big day," Erin said.

After talking, the group goes to the conference room to wait for the men to arrive with the minister. Erin and Nancy stay with Ashley and discuss the plans for a honeymoon as the time quickly passes.

Steele and Wagner arrive, bringing the minister with them.

"Where is Chuck?" John asks.

"We were in charge of the minister. Chuck was supposed to meet us here," Steele said.

As everyone was talking about Chuck's absence, Steele's phone rang.

"Okay, Wagner and I will be right over," Steele said into the phone. "Sorry, but we will be right back. It's an emergency."

The women enjoyed talking, and they didn't realize it was

already thirty minutes after the scheduled start of the wedding. The women go downstairs to find the cause of the delay. Ashley screams as they enter the conference room, "Where is Chuck?"

Her mother and Chuck's parents try to comfort her as Steele and Wagner return to the room.

"Where have you been? Did you find Chuck?"

"I'm sorry to tell you, Ashley, but a drunk driver hit Chuck's vehicle, and he is in the hospital. The Florida Highway Patrol is taking over the investigation, so we returned here to get you."

Ashley collapses into a billowy cloud of white tulle, crying. She is comforted by the women.

"Change your clothes, and Wagner, and I will take you to him. We can all go."

"No, I'm keeping my gown on, and we are going now. Bring the minister. He can marry us in the hospital," Ashley said while crying.

Her mother is comforting Ashley and attempting to calm her.

"Darling, the minister has already left. Let's go upstairs and change so we can see Chuck."

Chapter 59

FBI Special Agents Garcia and Santiago spent their first night at the hotel deciding the actions to take to solve this case. Choosing to see if they could hear the unidentifiable sounds the others claimed to have heard. They quietly sit in the main lobby, enjoying the orange flickering flames of the gas fireplace, when they hear strange sounds. They look at each other.

"What is that sound?" Santiago whispers.

"I don't know, but I'll record them with my cell phone."

They send the recording to headquarters later to see if somebody can identify the sound.

They spent the next day at the hotel searching for probable cause to get a warrant.

Walking down the main hallway, Garcia stops, listens at the ballroom door, and hears murmuring coming from the room. He tries to open the door and discovers it is locked, and the murmurs stop.

"That was strange. The noise stopped as soon as I tried the doorknob," Garcia said.

Garcia was walking down the hallway, tapping on the paneling, and found some of the wood, gave out a hollow sound, and motioned to Santiago. She listens as Garcia continues tapping on the wall. They agree it is time to report to Matt Murphy, the FBI special agent in charge. Hopefully, they have enough for a warrant.

While Garcia and Santiago searched for probable cause, Murphy looked into the hotel's owner. After searching many dummy corporations and checking overseas, he discovered that DD Investments LLC was the same corporation as the hotel's owner.

The FBI agent takes all the gathered information from Garcia and Santiago about the strange arrival of the Spanish-speaking housekeepers, their alleged debt, and the weird noises to the judge, who agrees there is enough probable cause to give them the warrant to check only the basement and ballroom.

All the agents gather to determine when and how to issue the warrant. They all agree that Steele and Wagner should be part of the team searching the building since they were the ones to discover the potential crime. The hotel is so old and extensive that they need enough men to explore it thoroughly. Since they will need a lot of boots on the ground, the FBI agent asks the sheriff for some of his deputies to help with the search.

"You can have all the men and women you need for this," the sheriff said. "Just solve this case."

"Yes, sir. We intend to solve it."

Murphy decided that Wednesday, Sept. 27, would be the day to conduct the search, giving everyone enough time to prepare and to obtain the FBI's mobile command headquarters. Also, more officers are working on Wednesday than on the weekend.

The location of the staging area is decided, the mobile command is made ready, and Murphy shows the men their assignments on a roughly drawn map of the hotel interior.

"Okay, everyone has their assignments. The camera operators are appointed to take the pictures, and the video operator is also named. Are there any questions?" Murphy asks. "Since there aren't any questions. You're dismissed. We will meet at 0600 on Wednesday."

Chapter 60

Everyone manages to calm Ashley and stop her sobbing.

"Ashley, let's go upstairs and change your clothes. You don't want that beautiful gown to get dirty," Ashley's mom said as she managed to get her daughter back to the bridal suite. She helps her remove the dress and hang it up. After quieting down, Ashley dresses in jeans, a blouse, tennis shoes, and a leather jacket. Her hair, full of curls, has fallen, giving her a wind-swept look.

Mother and daughter retreat to the main floor and the rest of the group. They all go to the hospital, and the nurse tells them that Mr. Vaughn is in surgery, and it will be a while before the doctor can give them some information.

The group settles down while Chuck's dad finds the vending machine and gets coffee for everyone, and Wagner helps carry the cups.

The group is sitting or pacing the room. No one is talking. Ashley is curled up in a chair and softly crying into her handkerchief.

Hours later, the doctor explains to the group that the surgery went as well as expected, and Mr. Vaughn is stable but will be in the ICU for a while.

"What kind of surgery did he have?" Ashley asks.

"He had a head injury, and we relieved the pressure on his brain and put him in a medically induced coma for a while."

"When can I see him?" Ashley asks with tears streaming down her cheeks.

"I've bandaged his head after the surgery. He's also on a ventilator, and his face is all bruised from the accident. You really shouldn't see him right now."

"I don't care. I want to see Chuck now," Ashley pleads.

"Please. Let her see him for a minute. It may calm her down," Ashley's mother said to the doctor.

"Alright, but just for a minute."

Erin goes with Ashley to see Chuck. They walk into the ICU and Ashley faints at the site of her fiancé. Erin, unable to hold her, lets Ashley slip to the floor. The nurses go to her and help Ashley onto a chair.

"It is such a shock to see Chuck like that. How long will he be in the coma?" she asks the nurse.

"The doctor said it would only be a day or two, depending on how well Mr. Vaughn is doing," the nurse said.

Erin helps Ashley return to the waiting room where her family and friends are waiting. Everyone is silent, looking with apprehension at Ashley.

"The doctor was right. I shouldn't have gone to see him. He looks so frail."

An FHP trooper walks into the waiting room and talks to Steele.

"We just checked on Mike Bowman. He is in critical condition, and the doctors are working on him. It appears Guy Hurtz was the driver, and he died at the scene. The medical examiner will give us his blood alcohol levels, but he was obviously drunk," the trooper said.

"How did the accident happen? Wagner and I weren't there long enough to check out the scene."

"From my preliminary investigation, vehicle one traveled eastbound on S.R. 40, and vehicle two was westbound. For an unknown reason, vehicle one crossed the median. The right front of vehicle one struck the driver's side of vehicle two, causing it to spin around and come to rest on the shoulder. Vehicle one came to rest in the middle of the westbound roadway, facing east."

"Which car was Chuck in?" Ashley asks.

"Chuck was vehicle two, and he was not at fault. I had the car towed to the body shop, and it looks totaled."

"Thanks for working the accident for us. We appreciate it."

"Not a problem. We always work together," the Trooper said as he left the room.

"Mike Bowman and Guy Hurtz were in the other car? You let them out of jail, and they almost killed Chuck?" Ashley said, beating her fists on Steele's chest. "This is all your fault."

"Now, Ashley, it's not Detective Steele's fault. Calm down," her mother said, helping her daughter sit down.

Chapter 61

At 6 a.m. Wednesday, the FBI special agents, Marion County sheriff's deputies, Steele, and Wagner meet at the staging area. The deputies are excited and hope to find enough evidence to stop a human trafficking ring. Everyone reviews their orders on where and what to search for to find evidence of human trafficking.

The FBI Special Agent in charge, Murphy, enters the hotel's front door with several deputies and asks to speak to the manager. Brenda Boyd, the manager, arrives at the front desk.

"What are you doing in here?" Boyd asks.

"Are you the one in charge here?"

"Yes. I am."

"Here is a warrant permitting us to search the basement and the ballroom. Please, stay out of our way."

"You can't do that. This hotel is private property."

"Yes, ma'am. This warrant says I can. Now, please step aside."

The group goes to the ballroom and finds it locked.

"Would you like to unlock the door, or should we break it down?"

"No. No. Don't break it. I have a key."

Boyd unlocks the door, and the men enter and see the room is arranged into twenty-one small areas, each containing a bed, a small bedside table with a lamp, and a folding three-panel room divider privacy partition between the beds.

"What is this?" the Special Agent asks Boyd.

"This is just a room we use when overbooked."

"I don't believe that is the truth, Ms. Boyd. How is this room actually used?"

"I'm not responsible for any of this. I'm just the manager."

"Arrest her on suspicion of human trafficking, read her the Miranda warning, and take her to headquarters. Maybe she will talk there," Murphy orders the deputy.

"Wait. You're arresting me on human trafficking?" Boyd asks. "I have nothing to do with that."

"Ms. Boyd, we are investigating a human trafficking ring, and you are our prime suspect. That is why the deputy is arresting you."

"Okay, men, keep searching," Murphy says commandingly.

A deputy handcuffs Boyd and reads her the Miranda warning.

"Do you understand your rights as I have read them to you?"

"Yes, I understand them."

The deputy takes her to headquarters to be charged.

The men continue searching every inch of the room. Steele notices one of the brass sconce lights is shiny while the others are tarnished. He goes to the shiny middle brass sconce light with the Swarovski crystal and wiggles the fixture, making it turn and causing the panel to open into a hallway.

"I found something interesting."

All the men gather at the opening and look into a long hallway. Steele carefully walks into the hallway and notices light bulbs hanging from the ceiling every six to eight feet apart. The narrow windowless passageway seems well-used, although some cobwebs are in the corners. There are doors on one side of the hallway. Steele opens one of the doors, and it opens into a regular guest room.

"This is interesting. I wonder why there is a secret door to enter the guest rooms?"

Steele continues down the hall and notices stairs going downstairs. He goes down the steps to discover another door at the bottom of the stairs. He opens it to a room of ten men drinking, smoking cigars, and talking. Each man has a young dark-haired woman wearing only a bra and panties on his lap or on a chair next to him

"FBI, everyone, stand against the wall and hold up your hands. Who is in charge?" Murphy said as he showed his badge.

The bartender comes from behind the bar, wiping his hands on a towel.

"I'm in charge here. What are you doing?" the bartender asks.

"This looks like you are running a brothel."

"No, sir, I'm just the bartender. I don't have anything to do with these women."

"Then who does?"

"Brenda Boyd, the hotel manager, takes care of the women, and Maria is the one who can talk to them. They don't understand English, and I don't speak Spanish. So, I don't get involved."

"Okay, get the officers in here and read everyone their Miranda rights and arrest all the men on solicitation of prostitution. Get Santiago in here and call for more female deputies to arrest these women for prostitution and get them to jail for questioning. Also, get them some blankets or something to cover themselves."

Everyone follows the FBI's instructions, and they call several buses to take everyone to jail. While continuing to search, they find another door next to the bar, which leads to a small room with the rest of the women and Maria.

"What are you doing sitting in this room?" Steele asks.

"We wait here until Ms. Boyd tells us they need more women, or we can go to bed," Maria said.

Murphy orders everyone to continue looking for evidence and has the prisoners transported to jail.

"Continue searching, and I'll go to headquarters and interrogate Brenda Boyd and find out what's going on here," Murphy said.

Chapter 62

Chuck's parents have been staying at the hospital to be with their son while he was in a medically induced coma. After two days, the doctors ordered them to go home for a while since there wasn't anything they could do there. They reluctantly agreed and went to their hotel to rest and shower. The next day, the doctor called to tell them that he felt Chuck was well enough to come out of the coma.

John and Barbara Vaughn immediately returned to the hospital in time to see the doctor remove the ventilator. Chuck is coughing but breathing on his own. The doctor is pleased with the results.

"We have slowly stopped the mediation, and he should be fully awake soon," the doctor said.

Barbara takes Chuck's hand and brings it to her lips.

"Hello, Chuck. How do you feel?"

"It may take a few more minutes. You have to understand Chuck will be confused, so give him some time. He might not remember the crash, and adjusting will take time," the doctor said.

Chuck lay on the bed, attempting to speak, but could not.

"Oh, Chuck, just rest. Dad and I will sit here with you until you feel better."

Ashley is at home suffering from a nervous breakdown and fatigue and is under the doctor's orders to stay in bed and not leave her home. Chuck's parents decide not to tell Ashley that Chuck is out of the coma and ask Erin and Nancy to keep her away until he feels better. Grant Steele has been giving Ashley daily updates on Chuck's recovery, but not all of the facts, as he wants her to get well before seeing her fiancé again.

They agree it would be in Ashley's best interest if Chuck's bruising went down slightly before she saw him again.

It took another two days before Chuck was able to speak, slowly.

"What happened? Where am I?" Chuck asks.

"Oh, Darling. A drunk driver hit you, but you are now on the mend in the hospital. Would you like to see Ashley?"

"Who?"

"Ashley, your fiancé. She's wanted to see you for the past few days, but the doctor wanted you to get better before she visited since she fainted the first time she saw you."

"I'm confused. I don't know what you are talking about. Tell me what happened."

Barbara continues talking to Chuck while John goes to the doctor and asks him about Chuck not remembering his fiancé.

"Amnesia can be part of the brain injury your son has experienced. Let's wait a while and see how he does. Don't pressure him into remembering. Let him remember on his own," the doctor said. "Maybe you could bring in pictures of her and tell him about her to help him remember."

Barbara talks to Chuck about Ashley and his life since he moved to Ocala. A day later, Chuck starts to remember and asks to see her.

When Ashley hears the news that she can see Chuck, she rushes to the hospital.

"Oh, Chuck. It is so good to see you doing so much better and out of ICU. How do you feel?" Ashley said as she gave Chuck a big hug.

"Oh, take it easy. I'm still sore. I'm doing better, but there are a lot of things that are still fuzzy. The doctor said it will all come back in time. I just have to be patient," Chuck said. "Did we get married?"

"No, we aren't married. A drunk driver hit your vehicle while you were on the way to the ceremony."

"Well, we will have to do something about that soon."

Erin and Nancy walk in just as Ashley screams in delight, talking about the wedding.

"Oh, Chuck, I was so worried," she said. "I just found you, my love, and I thought I would lose you."

"Well, everything looks much better than the last time we saw you," Nancy said.

"Now that Chuck is sitting up and remembers me and the wedding. Everything is fine," Ashley said, holding Chuck's hand.

Erin suggests that the wedding be held in the hospital as soon as possible.

"Getting a minister here and having a quiet ceremony with family and friends won't take much."

"Oh, Erin, that would be wonderful. When can we get this organized?" Ashley asks.

"Well, today is Tuesday. Why don't I get it together for Thursday? If that is okay with everyone."

"That would be wonderful," Ashley said.

Erin and Nancy contacted the hospital administration for permission to have the wedding in Chuck's room and requested the hospital minister. Plans proceed beautifully with everyone on board.

With the help of Erin and Nancy, Ashley dresses in her wedding gown and they help her get to the hospital. The staff arranged to hold the wedding in the hospital lounge for plenty of room.

As Ashley enters the lounge, Chuck's bed is in the center of the room.

"Ashley, you are beautiful. If everyone is here, let's get started," Erin said.

After the ceremony, the kitchen staff brings a cake for the celebration. Everyone is happy, but the nurse tells the group that

Chuck has to return to his room to rest, and the party is over.

"Now that you are happily married, I hope you are ready to go back to work," Steele said. "We are closing a big case I think you want to know about."

"You're right. It is time to return to work, but I will still need to spend time with my husband. Maybe I can work from here. I'll contact you next week, and you can tell me all about your big case," she says, glowing.

Chapter 63

Murphy, the FBI Special Agent in charge, arranges to interrogate the hotel manager, Brenda Boyd.

"What is going on at your hotel?" he asks her in the interrogation room.

"There isn't anything going on at the hotel."

"Then why do you have the locked ballroom filled with beds with wheels on them so someone can quickly move them and privacy screens?"

"I told you that is what we use when overbooked."

"Now, Ms. Boyd, a guest would not be happy in that setting, and we both know that. Just tell me what is going on."

"Where did you find the women? Why do you have them working as housekeepers and prostitutes? You're in big trouble, Ms. Boyd. But I don't want you. I want the man in charge of this human trafficking ring. Give me the big boss, and I will ask the D.A. to give you a deal."

"I can't tell you anything. If I talk, the boss will have me killed."

"We can protect you."

"No. You won't be able to save me from the boss. No one is safe from him."

While Murphy questioned Boyd, she asked for a lawyer. The other deputies interviewed all the men about how they knew about the brothel. They all said they heard about this place through word of mouth and the internet. Someone online told us it was a safe place to meet the women.

The women couldn't wait to tell their story and hoped they would be free. They all came over the border with the help of several predators, promising them a job and a place to stay for a price.

The victims came over as a group of families and good friends, but the predators took their money and valuable belongings. They split up the families and took the women and girls for prostitution. The girls were all teenagers. They saw the evil men take the rest of the families and beat those who were sick or unable to walk.

"The evil men told us that they would kill us and our families if we tried to escape before paying the huge ransom they put on each of us. That is why we continue to work for them. We don't have a choice," one of the women said in Spanish. "Our families paid them a lot of money just to come here. They took advantage of us. We just wanted to be free. The hotel lady forced us to have sex with those older men. We didn't want to do this. It is wrong."

After the deputies and agents completed the interrogations and filed their reports, the FBI agent in charge, Murphy took all the information to the district attorney so official charges could be made.

The D.A. informs Murphy that Bill Johnson from Johnson and Johnson Criminal Attorneys wants to make a deal for Brenda Boyd.

"How can she afford a high-priced lawyer like Johnson?" the Agent asks.

"It turns out he is doing it pro bono since his firm requires all the lawyers to do a percentage of their business to help the people who can't afford their services, and he knows this case will create a lot of publicity."

"Did he say what kind of a deal he wants?"

"He said Boyd will give us the boss and enough evidence to convict him of human trafficking and even more, but she wants immunity for any crime she may have inadvertently committed and be put in the Witness Protection Program," the D.A. said.

"I don't know about giving her complete immunity."

"Johnson said that is the only way she will tell you everything. I think it is a good deal if we can get the top man."

"Okay, let's hear what she says before we give her immunity."

The D.A. brings in the lawyer and Brenda Boyd to hear her information.

"David Drake is the man in charge of the human trafficking ring and has been doing this for years. He also owns the hotel, and it didn't take long to discover all its secret passages. The original owners built the hotel in 1920 during prohibition and built a speakeasy in the basement. I found the original plans for the building, and the owners put all the hidden passages to be built in the actual blueprints," Boyd said.

"How do you know all this, and do you have proof of what you are saying?" the D.A. asks. "Why were you making the women be prostitutes and laborers?

"I didn't have a choice. Drake found out I was skimming money off the top when he bought the hotel and said he would have me arrested if I didn't help him with his project. After his threat, I started collecting emails and recorded his calls about getting more people across the border. I needed insurance to protect myself if the cops ever figured out what was happening here," Boyd said. "I even have him on the phone saying he killed some contractor because he tried to stiff him, and he would do the same to me if I didn't follow his orders."

With the new information, the FBI took cadaver dogs to Drake's ranch and found the body of Barry Heron in a shallow grave near the barn.

The D.A. and Murphy agreed that if Boyd's evidence got them Drake, they would give her immunity and put her in the witness protection program.

Chapter 64

Ashley meets Steele in his office, and he hands her a hefty packet about the hotel and the human trafficking ring.

"Everything you need to know about David Drake is in the folder. He also killed Edward Moore to keep him and his horse from competing in the Derby. I guess he didn't count on the fact that he couldn't compete either since he didn't have a jockey for his horse."

"What about Sally? Did you find who killed her?"

"The D.A. is charging Mike Bowman with kidnapping and rape," Steele said.

"But how can you prove it? Sally is dead, and there aren't any witnesses."

"The doctors knew Sally was a rape victim, and they collected embryonic fluid from the womb before she died for a prenatal paternity test to prove the identity of the father of her unborn child. That is how the D.A. will win the case against Bowman," Steele said.

"What about the three boys that died in the accident?"

"Drake conned the boys into watching Helen Lane's boarding stable and report back to him. Then he told them to steal everything and take it to his ranch hands. The boys asked for more money, and Drake eliminated them as witnesses. He also wanted to put Sally in his prostitution ring, but she died."

"What happened to Sally Cobb's mother?" Ashley asks.

"She read about Sally's death in the paper, and she went out into the yard and started a fight with other inmates. She died from her injuries two days later.

"You are right. This is going to be a great story. You guys did a great job," Ashley said.

"Now that this case is closed, I can start looking for Whitey's missing daughter, Summer," Steele mumbled to himself.